GRAVITY

and Other Stories

CATHERINE PETROSKI

fiction international

Library of Congress Number:
81-71003
ISBN: 0-931362-05-9

First Edition

Acknowledgments: The following stories have been published previously: "John Gardner and the Summergarden," *Having Been There* (New York: Charles Scribner's Sons, 1979); "Life As the Wife of Khan & Khan," *Prairie Schooner* and *Ms.;* "Austin," *Prairie Schooner;* "Beautiful My Mane in the Wind," *North American Review* and *Ms.;* "A Wild Lens," *Mississippi Review;* "The Deposition," *University of Windsor Review;* "Creatures of This Place," *Virginia Quarterly Review;* "The Pump," *Cimarron Review;* "Gravity," *North American Review.*

Cover illustration obtained through special arrangement with Perkins Library, Duke University.

The author acknowledges the generous help of the National Endowment for the Arts and the Corporation of Yaddo.

fiction international, St. Lawrence University, Canton, New York 13617

For Henry

Contents

John Gardner and the Summergarden

Tonight I am holding my nose.

To talk to John Gardner.

He will answer the pay phone at the end of the bar at Gardner Gardens. I will ask him if my father is there because my mother wants to know but is tired and ashamed of calling the tavern herself. John Gardner will say, "Just a minute and I'll see," and then he'll put his hand over the phone for a second and come back and say, "No, I don't see him," and then still holding my nose like a long-distance operator and sounding stuck-up I will say, "Thank you, sir," and wait until he hangs up and then hang up myself, while my father is saying, "Thank you, John. I gotta be going."

Every night one of my jobs is to call Gardner Gardens. I can count on it. Weekdays, weekends, my father will be there when it's time for supper. At first it was fun, sort of, but now I can see why Mother doesn't want to call anymore, why she gave me the job. So for a long time now, I have been a different person every night. By now John Gardner must be pretty confused about why my father gets so many phone calls from so many different people.

What we all understand, Mother and Father and I, is that it's just a signal. We all know he's there. There's never any question. John

Gardner's saloon is only two blocks from our house and I used to ride my bike down to see if Father was really there, and he was. There are lots of saloons in town but if he went to another one it would just get all complicated. This way Father finds out when dinner is ready without starting a real fight about where he was hanging out. This way it's all in the neighborhood. John Gardner's tavern is down the hill past the Catholic church, just on the other side, in fact. The tavern has beer signs that work like magic and whiskey that nobody ever drinks and is full of the smell of old spilled beer and cigarettes. Out in back is a little fake brick building that's really one big barbecue pit inside. In the summer John Gardner's wife sells barbecued ribs and pork sandwiches there. And root beer and orange. There's a summer-garden, too, all screens, which they say is why it's called Gardner Gardens. In the summer John Gardner carries out beer in sloshy pitchers. I don't see how anybody drinks beer. It tastes like soap. I hate it.

Tonight, when I told Mother what John Gardner had said, she gave the lima beans a good, mean stir. "That man would lie to his own mother," she said, "if it meant selling another beer." She picked up the telephone and asked the operator for the number I had just called. But she hung up before John Gardner had had a chance to answer.

"Those front legs don't amount to much," Father said, looking at the pieces of squirrel on my plate. "What's the matter? Not hungry?"

He was trying to be nice, trying to make little jokes and be happy the way he does when he knows Mother's mad or he's stayed a little too long at Gardner's, which happens every once in a while. Mother doesn't think he's funny. I laugh a little to make him feel better and Mother stares at me.

"What's so funny?" she says.

"Daddy's funny." I don't know why I call him Daddy sometimes. He's Father.

"It's the beer, and that's not one bit funny," Mother says. "You'd think a person would try to get home when he's expected. After all I've gone through with the squirrels."

"Have to chase them down, Lou?" he asks. I giggle.

"You know what I mean. It's barely civilized."

"It was good enough for the pioneers," Father says.

"And the cavemen," I start to say, but Mother interrupts me.

"Well, it's ready," she says.

Dumb John Gardner, I think. Why does he have to go and sell Father all that beer that starts the trouble? What's so interesting about that smelly place with all those loud men? Father takes a head off the platter and puts it on his plate first thing.

"Now, this'll put hair on your chest," he says to me. He pries off the lower jaw and the little teeth glisten in their gravy bath. The big cutting teeth stay with the eyeless skull.

"Here," he says to me, and he puts the tongue on my plate next to the beans I wasn't planning to eat. It is a very small tongue. Mine grows fat in my mouth.

Father steadies the skull at the middle of his plate. The head is bare now. The cover of meat is gone.

"That's a good knife you've got there," Mother says and hands him another, an old one from the clubhouse. With the handle, Father cracks the case in one sharp blow and removes the brain.

"You can have the next one," he says to Mother.

"No thanks," she says, and she eats a forkful of mashed potatoes. I study the broken head on the edge of Father's plate. There are holes that were its nose.

The siren woke me up. Too low for the police, too high for the ambulance. It must be Snow White, the little white fire truck from the Twelfth Street substation. It stopped somewhere near. Then there were other sirens, police, the big trucks from downtown, an ambulance. It sounded like just down the street from us. I got out of bed.

Mother was flapping around in her scuffs and robe. Father was getting dressed. "What can you do?" Mother kept asking. "Don't you think you're just going to be in the way?" Father just kept getting dressed.

"Where is it? The Catholic school?" I wanted to know.

"Don't know," my father said. "It's somewhere close. My God, Lou. Look at the sky."

We looked and it was pink with smoke and light.

"You're being ridiculous. You're going to get hurt. You've got no business going down there. What can you do? You're just going to be in the way. Don't go. Please don't go." He was halfway off the front porch by then and just turned and yelled, "You stay here, now."

"Don't get close," Mother called after him.

I sat on the landing, afraid but wishing I could go too.

"Back to bed," she ordered. She turned and went to the kitchen.

In the morning it was as though nothing had happened. Father was eating his two slices of toast with damson plum jam and drinking his tomato juice and black coffee, reading the paper, not saying anything. My toast was waiting and already cold. "Tavern Gutted by Fire," the headline read. I could see it from my chair. Gardner's saloon was gone, just like that. The forever-falling waterfalls, the bounding spots of red and yellow and blue, the scenes of the North Woods lit from the back, the Southern swamps with their droopy trees. Destroyed, probably. And no place anymore for the loud music on the jukebox, and women smoking at the tables, slopping beer from pitcher to glass and from glass to mouth and maybe to the front of a dress, and yelling at kids whose noses needed wiping and whose hair was not combed and whose shoes were untied. The bad women, Father called them. The smell of spilled beer and stale smoke was gone, and now the new smoke.

My bike, Trigger, was damp with dew. I had left it outside leaning against the back porch. I had forgotten again to put it in the garage and if I rode away quickly they might not notice. The heavy smell of smoke and water hung all around. Through the schoolyard, up the hill. In everybody's open windows.

All that was left of John Gardner's was the remains of the brick walls and mounds of soggy junk. A man I had never seen before poked through the junk. The smell was awful.

The summergarden was safe. The giant cottonwoods and catalpas that surrounded it had been curled back by the fire, but the beer garden itself was the same as always. The paper Japanese lanterns caught a bit of the morning sun, and the pale colors danced in the east wind. I leaned Trigger against the side of the summergarden.

The screen door creaked. Along the walls stood the tables and benches. The summer jukebox was in place. I heard a stray cat stirring.

The stray cat turned out to be John Gardner. He was lying on his back on one of the benches. "What are you doing here?" he asked.

"Nothing. Just looking around."

"Everybody's looking," John Gardner said. "Not much to see, is there?"

I agreed. I told him I was sorry his tavern got burnt up. I wasn't sorry in one way, but I didn't tell him that. But in another way I was sorry because we could always count on Father's being at Gardner's. So I said just that we were sorry, especially Father, I guessed.

"I know," John Gardner said and coughed a little. He sat up on the bench and lit a Lucky. "That's right," he said as if he'd just remembered something. "That's right—you're the one's always calling for your pa to come home and eat."

"No," I lied.

But he stayed silent, his blue eyes distant. Old John Gardner wasn't even as old as Father. I could see him with the phone, tilting his yellow head to one side, going to Father, holding up one hand flat and pointing in its palm to the direction of the phone. I turned for the screen door.

"Hey, don't run off," he said. I looked back and felt very sorry for him. Now that the saloon was gone, what would he do? What would any of us do?

"I got a joke for you," he said. Sometimes Father brought home jokes with the homemade horseradish he got from somebody at John Gardner's. But Mother wouldn't let him finish the stories.

"That's okay," I told him. "I wouldn't get it anyway." Or so Mother always said.

"It's a clean joke, kind of," John Gardner said kindly. "You'll get it. You're the only one who might."

"Well, okay. Tell me."

John Gardner's face broke into a fat smile, the biggest smile anybody ever saw. With the hand that held the Lucky, he pinched his nose between his thumb and his fourth finger.

"Gardner Gardens," he said.

And we both laughed and laughed.

Life As the Wife of Khan & Khan

Khan sits across the table, folding and unfolding his hands. I tell myself it doesn't matter that one day he's Kubla, the next day, he's Genghis. Once I even thought he didn't realize the difference, or why he's like this, real and perplexing as his two selves may be to me.

When he looks up from the morning paper, the look is a granite glare. "What's *your* problem?" he demands. Without waiting for an answer he is back in the market for something with a strong dividend, camels, forges, fast horses, or so I think. So today we get Genghis, though minutes ago I could have sworn by what I took for an indulgent and beatific expression that today we would have Kubla, for a brief while at least. The expression must have had its source in last night's shishkebob or vine leaves or tabulah or the jug of wine that went with the pita.

"How could he have done such a thing?" Khan demands angrily, as he has many times of late. Again and again it's the same question, and it's a question Khan really doesn't expect, or want, me to answer. The *he* to whom Khan refers was his best-loved friend, a gentle man of milk-and-honey kindness and a fragile goodness. The *thing* he did was end his own life one spring morning, when to all the rest of the world his life looked like one infinitely promising ribbon of joy.

Khan is uneasy these days, and tosses in his sleep the nights since. Khan asks himself, Kubla has confided, whether he had been Genghis when he should have been Kubla to his dead friend. And the angrier Genghis grows and the more he demands an answer, the more certain Kubla is that there can never be answers to questions like those.

If all these years with Khan & Khan have taught me anything, it is that answering *ifs* and *whys* can waste tremendous amounts of time. The point now is, this day's sword already is drawn. Frightened children run for cover before the scourge of the east bedroom, Khan the Terrible.

"Why haven't you got your socks on?" he bellows at one of his children.

They scatter like leaves before the blast. They go into hiding inside their good manners, their compliance, their confused silence, their oatmeal. They are chameleon children, fitting offspring of Khan & Khan. It was somehow easier not long ago when the tray was on the highchair. It was much easier still in the swollen warm milky days and nights before the last child of this union was weaned. It was even easier than that in those dizzy days when we met and wed, making love all night, sleeping all day. But it was, if I am to be honest, easiest of all in those days before I saw his broad gentle face in the morning or heard him shout battle orders. Before I knew him either way it was an easier, more serene life, though in my loneliness at the time I could never have believed it. How was I to know that in the natural course of events the Khan's word-flowers would grow from the pale blossoms of fruit trees in the spring to autumn's purple death dahlias. My heart turns over to think of that change and our poor changling children. Our progeny learn the harsh curriculum of cruelty and destruction from this crazy Tartar, just as they struggle to learn of beauty and creation from the vestiges of the other Khan.

"What are you going to do today?" he asks me. I will wait for the rest of the question, which I know is coming. "Waste your time some more?"

There.

"Will you draw more worthless pictures of these worthless children?" He doesn't mean it, really, I tell myself. He can't mean it. He is not himself. Do I delude myself thinking that poor Khan can't help these wild swings? Aren't they the only way this poor man can deal with the still wilder swings of the world around him?

"No one will ever be interested in your silly pictures, you realize," he continues, as if he has never told me this before. "You ought to know by now that no one cares for them because they proceed from the particular to the universal, and not vice versa, and because they celebrate drawing for its own sake. Nobody really gives a shit about that kind of thing. Why don't you just take up photography, like everyone else? Don't you know yet what people are?"

I stop my ears with flattened hands. "Shut up, Khan, god damn you."

Perhaps it's a blessing I don't exactly remember the first drastic change; it simply happened. Up to that point it had been all pleasure domes between us, sweet breezes caressing the oasis we thought was love. Life was not life but silent swans and silk cushions, mosaics and alabaster, the whole lovely patchouli of earthly pleasures. It had landed in my very own lap. Khan, all the while, had folded and unfolded his hands. It was his habitual gesture, simple and sincere, I thought, like part of a meditative ritual. I took it as a sign of his patience with me and my own sometimes-extreme moods.

Day by day our reflecting ponds filled. The musk mallow came into blossom. The cork walls grew thicker, shutting out the outside world. There was nothing to fear. Things could go on like this, Kubla and I in our paradise, forever, amen. As it was in the beginning, things were unreal. On that day when we woke from our dream, Khan could see he had to get going, just as everyone does sooner or later. Day by day Kubla set out on his despised rounds, and day by day his occupation grew more onerous to him. Kubla, Kubla.

Kubla, little boy inside the big boy, soft hands that learned to grow hard, how difficult that knowledge must have been for you. What was the cost of that lesson that taught you to work against the world that worked against you? And was it all the harder learning these lessons late? However much I love dear Kubla, the creator of our children, night's honey whisperer and stroker of love-weary thighs, however much I want alone that sweet and noble Khan, I know it is not possible. Kubla himself would be utterly dead, like his dear irretrievable friend, had he not found the protection of Genghis. Snarling, swearing, downright mean Genghis, the aggressor, makes others uncomfortable that he may reach his ends. He is a human predator. Where and how did you learn to play the role of beast, Kubla? Why and how do you swallow and kill gentle words alive, terrible Genghis?

I know, of course, just as he knows, exactly how and why it had to come about: that once in blind idealism, Khan underestimated an adversary. Kubla very nearly got his throat cut. It was a frightful, ugly battle, not because Kubla fared so poorly but because it was not fairly fought. Khan's old friends, seeing the swing of events, fled, saving themselves. In the din of that battle, Genghis was born, writing his new laws. Never underestimate the power of a coward, he wrote. Never underestimate the value of stupidity. Never assume the right things will be done for the right reason. Never count on anybody but yourself. These are the new code of Khan, the secrets of his success, the order of his worship. Without the secrets Khan learned in that blood bath there would be no pleasure dome at all, no froth to decorate our life, perhaps not even life itself. The daily rounds of ravaging, repulsive as they are to Kubla and to me, are now our daily bread.

Genghis' coming, I admit, cooled Kubla's sun, and with it the fire of our love. The alabaster of our hermitage grew clammy to the touch. Genghis' birth left scars across our eyes. The mosaic gapped and caught common dirt in its cracks. Beneath the marble floors a fault threw the once-smooth slabs into polished escarpments. The espaliers refused to grow as they were bade, wanton vegetables. Kubla, poor Kubla, would cry miserably for his missing innocence, his open eyes, his generous and gentle heart. And then as quickly Genghis would snarl, forswearing those idealistic, misspent years. "My god," Genghis would rant, "think of the *time*!" At times like those I sit quietly, even motionless, not wanting to inflame him with so much as a movement. Any movement might be construed as a move against him. I know better than to risk such a misunderstanding. And perils like those are the occupational hazard of being wife of Khan & Khan. The sun cools over our desert, a waste in which it seems we are the only two survivors. Or three.

They do look alike, the two Khans, that much I must say. From our infancies, we've all heard it said: Appearances are everything, and nothing. And we've all heard it said: A ruler is, after all a ruler. It appears that a Khan is a Khan is a ruler, after all. But when Khan and I journey to the shopping oasis (incognito, of course), we hear the beggars asking among themselves the question no ruler wants to hear: When is a ruler not a ruler? Khan in his date-picker's get-up and I in my potter's smock ask the fakirs the same question, and they answer our question with other questions. When Khan asks about his dear dead friend, the fakirs turn away and pretend not to have heard.

Weary of shopping, Khan and I gather our purchases and strap them behind the horses' saddles. Well, the old pleasure dome may be going to seed, but it is home. The noise of the market fades behind us as we make our way out into the sands. We let the horses walk, and talk of rules and rulers and fakirs and friends.

"How did that go, what that blind fakir said?" Khan asks me. The urgency of his question disguises which he is. "Didn't he say, 'Does a ruler stop being a ruler when he falls off his horse?'?" It is Kubla, tentative, questioning. "What do you suppose that means?" he asks.

The horses deal with the sandy incline by sliding down on their haunches. We all collect ourselves and Khan goes on, recalling more of the fakirs' words. " 'Does a ruler cease to rule when his Maker goes into an opium sleep?' one of them said to me. An odd metaphor, don't you think?"

"Perhaps a ruler stops being a ruler when he loses his socks or when his harem rebels or his children ignore him." I wonder how I could say such a cruel thing. The horses' heads bob on. Tiny silver bells on their bridles ring in the chill evening.

"Rubbish! If his troops mutiny. Or if all his sheep and camels sicken and die. Or if his temples collapse. That's when it's over! Now be quiet, woman." Genghis turns his head from me and asks his horse to canter.

No, Khan & Khan, I think, I would tell you but I don't have to, because we both know it. The only time a ruler is no longer a ruler is when he ceases to think of himself as a ruler. Then, and only then, is his admission confirmed by his scrawniest cat, who will turn its back and lift its tail in arrogant salute. Then and only then the patchouli and musk mallow give it up, as your dear friend did, and drift on to some greater pleasure dome, another bower of alabaster and silk and dirt and weed.

My clever mare keeps her distance from Khan's unpredictable horse, which for once has had the good sense to settle into a quiet lope, as we are still some distance out. Khan knows I am his as he is mine, and I in turn know he will rave and swear and shout, then play upon the lute. That is the beauty of the beast. He will terrorize our children, then swoon like a puppy in my bed. He will throw his dirty socks against the wall, then take out the trash and do those things for which I have neither the stomach nor the strength. He will mutter in his nervousness, rant in his frustration, excoriate the stupidity surrounding him, then sing songs of spring and rains and tenderness in the moonlight, folding and unfolding his hands. I will be as many wives to as many Khans as Khan can be, just so long as he is more than one.

Together Khan & Khan and I watch the days, loaded with shapes of people, tear past like a rush-hour express, and we do nothing to stop them, for we can do nothing. About that I would not have Khan & Khan worry. And of the trains that have passed I would not have him regretful, since those are shapes and days that cannot be called back.

Austin

Last night after the show closed up at twelve on the dot Binny give me something special in his trailer. I could tell he was holding something behind his back so as I couldn't see it so I guessed he was hiding a surprise for me. He teased me like he always does, making fun of me because he says I'm just a kid that doesn't know anything but I know he's only playing that way. What he give me was a pretty seashell necklace, only Binny told me right away that it wasn't exactly a sea shell like most. It's pink, nice shiny plastic, and it hangs on a silverish chain round my neck and I don't think I'll never take it off cause it's from Binny and it was a real surprise.

Anyway Binny must have read up on that little sea shell that isn't a sea shell cause he told me all about what kind it was. Called a sand dollar, Binny said. That the real ones are little animals that live in the sea. How they're supposed to break, the real ones, and out flies supposed to be five doves for peace. How they're really sea urchins, them little animals, just like you, he said. And that made me feel kind of bad for a minute. So I said to Binny, this one's better than a real one cause it won't break like that. Binny laughed and said maybe we could try finding a real one and break it open and see what happens when we get to Corpus. Last year when the show was in Corpus

I was where I used to call home. I never been there, Corpus. I didn't even know the show or Martha or Binny was alive last year.

Binny said, it is right pretty. It'll go with all the pink clothes you got, he said, and that pearly pink nail polish I got the Saturday before I left what used to be home. Binny laughed when I said that I didn't never want to take off the sand dollar, and said, don't never say never. But Binny will see I'm wearing it and maybe he will know I'm wearing it to say thank you for being so nice.

This Austin here is a pretty town and where we're at on the lake front is a real pretty spot. Not like Dallas where we was all hemmed in by old buildings that must have looked real modern once upon a time. That fairground has some nice things, like its aquarium. It's real dark there and you can watch the fish glowy in their tanks. And the splotchy harbor seals, but they have cataracts on their eyes like grandma and that ruined the aquarium for me. But I like this much better. Out in the open like, with the lake and the sky and lots of clean air and friendlier people. A lot of people just aren't nice to folks with the traveling shows. Call us carneys and treat us like we aren't human beings. Like my folks never let me go when we was at the State Fair once. I was little then and I can only remember so many people I never saw before. It wasn't a good time but it seems like we never had a good time together cause we was always worrying about what's next. Which is why I left after we had a bad fight and why I joined the show. The people here don't seem to worry much about the next thing —the next day, the next town, the next anything. They just take it like it comes.

Sometimes I guess I get to missing them because I guess I should miss home like in all the songs and I get to feeling lonesome. Even though there's Martha, who I work for and who's been real good to me. And Binny. But if you got to be lonesome Austin is a nice place to be it cause this here lake is real pretty. They call it Town Lake I guess because the town is around it but it ain't really a lake. It's really some river, and last week when we was setting up they found a man floating in it. I seen them drag him out. They put him on a stretcher all blue and grey and took him away one afternoon about three o'clock. And nobody knew who he was cause there wasn't nobody missing in particular. When it happened with the ambulances and police and all, Binny just about had his spin-art stand ready to go and Martha had me blowing up balloons until I was blue in the face. Just like any other time we set up for a stand, all day metal hitting metal over at the rides. But finding the man did make it a little different. I was glad for the break, but it was sad about the guy they found in the river. Even the guys on the rides got to stop work for that.

Spring is funny, I told Martha, but she acted like she didn't hear and maybe she didn't. She's getting older and sometimes people that old can't hear. Sometimes they can, too, and pretend when it's convenient not to hear. But I guess Martha didn't want to talk about spring. You look across the lake and see the fruit trees blooming out like that and redbuds and grass all bright and green and even though it's pretty, somehow it can make you sad. Maybe that's why Martha didn't answer. And things go on and on, always balloons to blow up, darts to keep putting feathers on. Martha's been doing it a long time. You got to wash your hair, go to the laundromat, do your bunk, then you get to thinking, What if I didn't.

But now it's getting on to evening and the night is when we make most of our money. The lights attract the people like moths, Martha says. It's you that gets people to play Martha's game, Binny says. I don't know if I'll last as long as Martha. She's been in this business for forty-three years this coming June. But Martha says it's just like anything else. You do your job, you make your money, she says. Sometimes you're happy, sometimes you're sad. Sometimes you win, sometimes you lose, she says. Being a carney doesn't make you different from other people, Martha says. She says regular people think we're all cheats and sharps, but Martha says carneys aren't any more that way than anybody else. Everybody cheats somewhere along the line, and most more than me, Martha says. Martha reads the papers and always listens to the news. Binny told me Martha's fixed real good, that she knows about the stock market, the one in New York. That old gal could buy and sell us all, Binny told me. What I really would like is to stick with Binny, but he says, You stick with her and you'll do all right. After all, Binny says, all he has is a spin-art trailer, fifty cents a shot, and a 1957 Harley that don't start, but Martha's got a balloon game and knows a lot about people. Binny is a funny guy. He laughs and says the spin-art stand will come and go, but the balloon game will last forever. I hope it don't rain tonight.

There is this guy with a camera and I can't figure him. At first I thought he was taking pictures of his little girl on the pony ride.

Then a lady asked him, why are you taking a picture of my little girl? and then her husband asked him, how'd you like somebody to bust that Nikon, boy?, so then he moved on away from the pony ride, around the back of the merry-go-round and down one side of the midway, the other side. He was a funny-looking guy, almost looked like an Indian. Not a redman, but an Indian Indian. He had long hair in a ponytail but it was thin like him and clean so as you'd hardly notice it was long. I could keep an eye on him all the way down the midway he was so tall and he was looking for somebody else to take pictures of I guess and he must of found some because he really took a long time to work his way around to the balloon stand. He stopped for a while at Binny's spin-art, I could see that. He looked at the samples Binny had tacked around the top and looked into the painting holes that Binny lines with fresh foil every morning of the world and I guess he looked at Binny. He might of taken a picture of Binny cause he really seemed interested in Binny's stand. But probably what really held him up was old Okie. Maybe not Okie himself, cause I couldn't see if he went in to see him, but how everybody stood around listening to the swampman pitch. Like to be hypnotized. I don't know if the camera man would even be allowed in, with that camera slung on his neck. Anyway when he come around by here, I felt like asking him if he wanted to take my picture but I didn't because I had already figured out that that was the odd thing about his pictures. You weren't supposed to know he was taking them.

As he come by the balloons he stopped for a minute to listen to Martha, far away in the middle of the alley. She called out to him, but he acted like he don't hear. Like most.

You know Binny has red hair and he says that's why he has such a short temper. But this afternoon the fellow come around again with the camera with the ponytail. And instead of taking Binny's picture again, he took mine while I wasn't looking and Binny saw it and got mad. Called the camera man a hippy and said I was being used. About fifty times. And asked me if I enjoyed being used.

Binny's been saying that a lot lately. He says how everybody uses me. That Martha uses me. He says if Martha stood in the balloon booth maybe people would look after they heard her spiel but once they took a look at her, they wouldn't pay no attention. Never play. Maybe Binny's right. I tell Binny what my grandma said, the one with the cataracts. One hand washes the other, she always said. I use Martha, she uses me, only I never said that right out, just the thing about the hands. That's how the world goes around, I told Binny. Binny didn't laugh and said I was too young to be a cynic, but I don't get his meaning. It probably wasn't good. Binny has his moods.

So when Binny gets like that, I get mad and tell him off, like I don't know how he can sit around with all them catsup squirters of paint, trying to get people to do that silly spin painting. Course I just say that when I'm mad at him. Really I think the spin paintings is pretty, some of them after you practice. Binny can make beautiful ones, but when he's in one of them moods I won't tell him that.

What made the fight worse was I brought up going to look at the azaleas. Thought it would help. We would get over our fight. Binny told me we should stay with our own kind, but I kept going on how one of the girls told me the azaleas was blooming in the rich part of town. How she told me all about how to get there and I asked Binny would he take me there some morning when we was all ready. So Binny blew up and said, don't you even know enough to stay out of where you're not wanted, and don't you even know enough not to want things you can't have, and don't you even know enough to keep with your own. Don't go getting any ideas, Binny told me. Which confused me cause I always thought Binny had lots of ideas that didn't necessarily work out. And which got me real mad back cause it's a free country and the roads is public, after all, which is just what I said to Binny. But there ain't any arguing with Binny. If he guesses you might win the argument he stomps away. Says you're a kid, and what do you know.

It didn't come to that this time, but no, Binny said, no. I ain't taking you to any rich part of town to look at azaleas. Just a bunch of ugly pink flowers in ugly green tubs, he said. Said he wouldn't have such an ugly color as them in his catsup squirters. Said the reason he really hates them is they don't grow natural, that them plastic tubs is the only reason they grow, that the ground here ain't right, that it's all artificial. Just look across the lake, Binny told me, at them fruit trees growing natural in the ground. That ought to be good enough, Binny said, cause that's the best you can get.

So I did. I didn't say no more about driving out to see no flowers, and all them trees budding out across the lake was pretty and I remembered what I heard about what was over there and asked Binny if it was true there was an animal shelter over there. Just to make conversation. It was the Humane Society, he told me, over by some baseball fields. I told him the baseball fields didn't hold any fascination to me but maybe could we go on a walk to the Humane Society some morning.

Well, that was how it all started, with Binny saying people used me. I don't get the connection. So after the fight with Binny I went in Martha's trailer where I live and put on my pink silky top that looked nice with the sand dollar and combed my hair nice and brushed my teeth and put on some nice perfume somebody I don't want to remember give me once, and that almost spoiled everything for me, and then without thinking too much or looking back to see if anybody was watching me go, I started walking by myself across the bridge and then turned left down to where the Humane Society ought to be if I figured right.

I got about half way there and here comes Binny. What you think you're doing, girl, Binny asks me. Taking a walk, I say. He knows perfectly well what I'm doing, where I'm going.

You going to the Humane Society, he says. Could be, I say. Martha sent me looking for you, Binny says. She says she needs you to go get change. Binny looks at me funny, then he says, you coming with me, half asking, half telling.

Well, I say, if Martha needs me, guess I better. And when we got back, Martha told me to stick around when there was work to be done.

If you say everybody uses me, I asked Binny this afternoon, what about you, Binny? He looked at me for a long time, funny. Didn't answer. So I asked him again, and finally he said, if I was using you, would I tell you about it?

Then he got up and left.

Shut down the sides of the spin-art and just took off, like that. He was gone about forty minutes. I didn't see where he went, what he took with him. But when he come back, he had something stuck into the front of his jacket. Pretty soon I could see it was something alive, moving in there. Made me think of a mare about to foal. Then I knew where he had been. I knew he was over to the Humane Society.

Here, Binny said, here. This is how I use you. Go on, he said, it's for you. He opened up his jacket and pulled out a puppy all fluffy and white.

It's yours, he said. From Binny. I gotta get the spin-art open now. And just like that Binny left. I can't figure him out, he's such a funny guy, but he sure give me a nice puppy. Just a mutt, I guess, but going to be a pretty dog. So now I know for sure Binny went to the Humane Society for me, got me this dog, and give him to me, like the sand dollar. Except I can't wear the dog.

Well, he ain't going to live in no trailer with me, Martha said. You might just as well take him right back to that Humane Society or whatever it was where that crazy Binny got him. Martha was hopping mad. She was all red in the face. Her voice got hoarse. I never seen her in such a fit.

Why, Martha, I asked her. I don't see no reason for her to take on so about a little dog. Somehow it don't seem right. But asking her why only made her all the madder. Just let me tell you why, Martha says. I never lived with no animal yet and I ain't about to start now. And, she says, that's final.

He's already broke, Martha, I tell her, and look how scared he's got. But it didn't do no good talking to Martha about the dog. She wouldn't have none of him, and told me if I was to keep on in the balloon game and being her helper and all the dog would have to go. She said I'd either have to take him back to the Humane Society or give him to Binny to take care of. And, Martha said, let off with that Binny while you're at it.

Which surprised me kind of. So I don't know what I'm going to tell Binny. Can't tell him about how nasty she got, especially about him, how she called him a redhead hippy and a misfit and the things she said about his spin-art, how it was ugly and silly and he was nuts with his foil linings and catsup bottles and how it wasn't even really any fun for the people.

And I couldn't get a word in edgewise. While she was at it she said some awful things, things about me, not that I never heard them things before just not from her and where I heard them before I left, and the worst part is she said them just to hurt because she knows for a fact they aren't true. About Binny and me. Binny says some things, kidding like, but they don't really hurt, and when he says I don't know nothing, that's different than what Martha said. And I got to thinking, Binny's said some not nice things about Martha, but my grandma always told me, the one with the cataracts like the seals, have a good word for people and they'll have a good word for you. It didn't turn out that way with Martha. I always thought grandma was the smartest best person in the world. And then Martha too. Sometimes people no matter how smart you think they are make some bad mistakes. Sometimes they say such bad things there's no going back, and things are never the same after. After something like that happens, there's no trusting anybody. You never know when they're going to hit you with something else. It's not worth it. There's no erasing it, like somebody spit on the chalk and wrote up a blackboard. And now I feel sad, like the same thing's happened with Martha happened with my family, and though I'm still sitting here in my bunk in her trailer it's like I'm not here at all.

There's nothing else for me, and I can't leave Martha. Binny said it. Nobody'd come if it wasn't for me. I'm the draw and it's Martha's booth.

It's cold today and looks like all the blossoms on the trees is going to blow away, clean off the trees. It rained last night, the way it does around here: one minute it's hotter than Hades, the next comes up a big blue-grey cloud down the plains and you can see the cold in it coming. The wind starts in blowing, slow at first, then faster and faster. And you can see the leaves turn themselves over in the wind. The sky gets maybe half dark and then it comes, big drops. Not anything easy or half-noticeable, but big loud drops of rain. Sometimes it stops just as fast as it starts, but last night it kept up for a time. And then this morning it was cold and grey, but it doesn't really bother me that much. I'm going some place in a little while.

When the rain started in last night, Binny come over by the balloon booth and I was gathering up darts. Looks like there won't be much doing now, he said, and I looked and the spin-art was locked up tighter than a drum.

Guess not, I say. So I have to tell him about the dog, but before I get even a chance, Binny looks at me funny and says, What you name that little dog? almost like he could read my mind.

That scared me some, and instead of telling him that I had to give it back or that we had to take it back, that Martha wouldn't let me keep him, I say instead to Binny and I don't know why, I ain't given it much thought.

Then Binny says to me, I was thinking we ought to name him

something so we could put something on this. Binny reached in his pocket and pulled out a tag and handed it to me. MY NAME IS and there was a blank and I BELONG TO and another blank. To fill in the names. I couldn't look at Binny just then. The little dog was chewing the leg of Binny's pants, but Binny didn't pay any mind to what he was doing. I guess then Binny could see I was trying not to cry.

Now what you crying for, Binny said, you never pulled that before. That I seen, he said. The trouble was you never know how much to tell a person. So I didn't know what to say, whether he ought to know about Martha and the bad things or just about the dog or about how nothing was coming true for me in my life about good words and such, all the things that weren't ever supposed to be changed. Or even did the dog have to go at all, since Martha and all weren't what I thought. It would be the end of Martha, sort of. It might be the end of Binny. It might be the end of both. Maybe the Humane Society would take me too. I seen things end before.

Things already ended around here. Cause things won't ever be the same with Martha and me, even if I live in her trailer for the next forty-three years, not after everything that happened. Austin, I tell Binny. We can call the little dog Austin, where we are, I said. I don't know why I done that, it made my head feel light.

That's a real good idea, Binny says. We can have the tag filled in, Binny says, maybe tomorrow morning cause there's not going to be much doing around here with this cold front coming through. And I got a little collar for Austin, Binny says, fishing in his jacket pocket. And a leash too, he says.

Binny looks at me funny, trying to figure out what I'm thinking, I guess. I mean, he says, it's your dog and it's o.k. to put the collar on him, ain't it? So I tell him sure it's o.k.

Binny keeps talking, talking. Talking more than I ever heard him. Binny's talking through my thoughts. I hear him but I don't understand him. I'm thinking and what I'm thinking is there's never nothing. One thing ends, another starts up, like them trees across the lake. Some things is nicer than others, that's for sure. But there's always something.

You know you had a right good idea there, naming the little dog Austin, Binny says. That way we can remember when we was in Austin. You still wearing that sand dollar, he says.

And Binny holds out his hand with the MY NAME IS tag and

looks at me different like. Binny's face looks glad. And Binny says, you keep this for now, o.k., cause I might lose it or get paint on it, o.k., and when he give me the tag to take care of it was different than with the sand dollar, which wasn't real, and his hand touched mine kind of long.

With Alda at the Outer Banks

From all the way across the Hatteras Seaside Restaurant a young woman stares at my husband. I know why. "Alan Alda, right there," she whispers to her girlfriend across the table, and she tilts her head our way and points with her eyes.

Even at this distance I know what she is saying. I can read lips, at least lips that form the words *Alan Alda.* I've had practice. On Park Avenue and Michigan, at Kennedy and O'Hare, in theatre lobbies everywhere and twenty-four hour grocery stores in the Carolina Piedmont (where we now live), these cases of Mistaken Identity happen more and more frequently. Everyone thinks she's found Alda. Invariably it happens on the highway, as it did on our way here to the Outer Banks, where we've come this weekend to see the Hatteras Light before it falls into the sea. Passing cars slow, then "Look! It's Alan Alda!" will come through clear as day, even with two sheets of glass between us, and the roar of eight radials and two tape decks masking all human utterance.

"Someone else is doing it," I whisper to my husband, who is busy shelling his last fresh cold shrimp. "The two School Marms, second booth from the door."

"Two School Marms!" he says, faking total shock, "Doing it here?

In front of everyone?" He leers and I check the ceiling. Until people started accosting him for his autograph, he maintained that any resemblance between him and Alda was a figment of my imagination; now he's not so sure. I tell him it's his manner, his bearing, his New York way of talking, plus the slight but very real likeness. Any woman who thinks she's found Every Woman's Dream Man is going to ignore the dissimilarities, of which there are many. Take their smiles—"Please," the look-alike would say, like Henny Youngman. While Alda's grin is ear-to-ear, my husband smiles carefully, not willing to expose too much of the full set of caps installed after he totalled his first two-wheeler in Brooklyn's Prospect Park, thirty years ago. But here in Carolina, he smiles and gives his expert diagnosis. "You're cuckoo."

"You've got his accent down pat," I point out.

"This is the way I always talk."

"Dis is duh way I ohlways towk."

He looks hurt. "I'll stand up and they'll forget this Alda-business." He is convinced he is taller than Alda, though neither of us has seen statistics. "Six-three is too tall for a stand-up comic," he says. "Besides, my eyes aren't blue."

About the eyes, he is right, but six-three is no Wilt Chamberlain. "But your hair *is* bushy *and* greying *and* cut just like Alda's."

"No, his is like mine. For the record, *you*'ve been cutting my hair like this. Since grad school, which was long before anybody ever heard of Alan Alda." Outflanked, I ponder the fantasy: my Delilah to Alda's Samson! "I think it's a conspiracy," he says, and he beckons the waitress. "Let's walk some of this shrimp off."

"I didn't know he wore glasses," one of the School Marms is saying as we pass their table on the way out. It's a struggle not to punch the Idol in the ribs.

Though he might not like my taking notice, the ersatz star has begun to enjoy the stares. Whether or not he actually cultivates the illusion is—like the haircut—a question of Who Looks Like Whom, The Chicken or the Egg. The unruly forelock, the olive fatigues, the relentless turtlenecked and tweeded pursuit of casual chic—we're lucky he's not into stills and martini-drinking. He wears an ERA/ YES button, tutors our son in pizza-making, and nurtures our daughter's love of math. He cries at the sad parts of movies, encourages my pursuits, does the dishes, even attends feminist rallies. Watching M*A*S*H reruns, our children laugh wildly as they glance back and forth between TV and daddy.

Yesterday on the road between Chapel Hill and Nag's Head, we noticed more than the usual number of passing, slowing cars, with cargoes of gaping, sometimes gesticulating motorists. No one car could have so many flats, we decided. "Look! Another one!" the children chorused, "They think you're Alan Alda, Daddy!"

"Just shut up, back there." He tries so hard to sound gruff. "It's just someone's underwear hanging out of our trunk. I know you kids, anything for a laugh. What did you tie to the back bumper this time, the neighbor's dog?" Slowing cars, staring people, and hysterical denials from the rear seat continued all the way to the shore. Finally at the resort, the beaming desk clerk proffers pen and registration card, then appears puzzled by what my husband writes.

"Has anyone ever mentioned, sir," the clerk ventures, slyly giving wife and kids the once-over, "that you bear an uncanny resemblance to a certain actor?"

"It happens all the time," my husband smiles, and I cringe as he ventriloquizes through his caps, *very* clearly, "Charlie Chan." In his rush behind the mailboxes, the clerk forgets to give us our keys. He is whispering we-know-what to the switchboard operator.

As if by magic, the manager appears. "Your key, sir," he intones, and the clerk and operator peer around for another look as the manager solemnly assures Charlie Chan that the Inn's guests can count on privacy.

So here we are, walking off the shrimp, hugging each other's waists as we pad barefoot on the flat wet sand at the water's edge. Hollywood itself couldn't have staged a more beautiful weekend at the Outer Banks, this year or any other. Theatrical clouds tower in the clear, high blue skies; a warm sun shines, and the onshore breeze whips up a surf sedate enough for children's play but with enough pizzazz to recall *From Here to Eternity* and the benchmark love-scene of our teenages. All we need is a Johnny Mathis ballad.

"Too bad about the Hatteras Light," I say. I feel attached to the black-and-white spiral-painted landmark we visited that morning, for though *I'd* never seen it before, a sea-captain ancestor had steered home to New Bern by it. "You think they'd find some way to save it."

"Erosion is an Act of God," my husband says, uncharacteristically philosophical, then adding quickly, with a Groucho leer and the roll of an imaginary cigar between his empty fingers, "but I like 'em passive better." I groan. "The eyes could be managed, you know," he continues. "Blue contacts."

"What?"

"Alda's eyes. They're blue. I could get blue contacts."

"They usually don't prescribe contacts for *children,*" I giggle. "But would it help if I picked up a scrub-suit for you at the Med School store?"

"What? And have you stencil it S*H*A*M? No, you'd put H*A*M*S, I know you. Tell everything you know." He eyes me for a second. "Say, how about H*A*S*M?" He does Groucho eyebrows, up and down. "No, the whole thing's too stagey. I'd look like someone who looks like Alan Alda trying to look like Alan Alda."

"You've got it," I agree, but I relish the picture of the look-alike lecturing his media manipulation class wearing hospital greens.

"*Excuse me,*" calls a voice, female, over the waves' roar. "I just couldn't help coming up and introducing myself and saying hello...." Her every vowel says New York. She is about our age, I notice—old enough to know better—and sounds just like my sister-in-law, pure Brooklyn.

I steal a glance at the look-alike: he is braced for this familiar encounter. But something tells me this time it will end differently. I guess I always knew the moment of untruth would have to come, sooner or later. My husband has come to terms with the fate that goes with his face. I read "autograph seeker" in his eyes, his *hazel* eyes. Yes, he will say, of course, happy to.

Alan Alda, he will write. No flourishes, sensible, sane, perhaps a slight ironical backslant, self-contained, a graphologist's paradigm. And above all, legible.

"This is going to sound like a *really* weird question," the woman disclaims, all big city wariness.

"That's okay," beams the genial star of television's longest running comedy series, 1000% understanding. "Go ahead."

I can't possibly play this supporting role with a straight face. Suddenly our children's welfare in the waves concerns me overwhelmingly, so I must excuse myself and rush off. I try to concentrate on the sound of the breaking combers, the thought that Hammacher Schlemmer sells this very noise to relax people, and the awful fact that I can't make out more than an occasional word. After only a minute or so, the two of them exchange pieces of paper quickly and the woman leaves abruptly. The look-alike, looking stunned, wanders up to where we are toying with the Atlantic Ocean.

"Look at this, will you?" He hands me Mr. and Mrs. Something-Something with a Brooklyn address, the paper limp with salt spray. "I said we could have a drink at 5:30, okay? She went to find her husband—we all went to school together, seventh grade, back in Park Slope." He is overjoyed, and seems relieved. "And guess what she said. She told me that Alan Alda has always reminded her of me. What do you think about that!"

I lick his salty ear and whisper, "Incredible!"

Beautiful My Mane in the Wind

I am a horse, perhaps the last mustang.

This is my yard, this is my pasture. And I told her I hate her. My dam-mother. She does not understand horses. She doesn't even try. There are many things she doesn't notice about me.

Horses move their feet like this.

Horses throw their heads like this, when they are impatient, about to dash away to some shady tree. See how beautiful my mane in the wind.

Horses snort.

Horses whinny.

Horses hate her.

I am a girl horse. I am building a house under the loquat tree. It is taking me a long time.

My house is made of logs, logs that Daddy doesn't want. That is because our fireplace goes nowhere. It is just a little cave in the wall because this is Texas and it is mostly hot here. Our fireplace has a permanent fake log. I am six.

I will be six next month.

Anyway that is why I got the real logs when our weeping willow died and Mama pushed it over one Sunday afternoon. The bottom of the trunk was rotten and the tree just fell over and Mama laughed and the baby laughed and I didn't laugh. I hate her.

I hate also the baby who is a Botherboy.

Daddy cut the willow tree into pieces I could carry and gave them to me and now I am building a horsehouse under the loquat and waiting for a man horse to come along, which is the way it is supposed to happen.

I saw a picture of one and its name was Centaur.

Of a Sunday afternoon, in her stable

My room I also hate. Bother loves it best and squeals when he gets to its door, because he thinks it's nicer than his own room, nicer than the bigroom, nicer than anyplace at all. He likes best all the blocks and the toy people. I build temples and bridges sometimes but then he comes along. He throws blocks when he plays because he's just a baby. And a boy. And not a horse.

What I hate most about this room is picking up pieces of the lotto game when he throws it all over, picking up pieces of jigsaw puzzles that he has thrown all over. Picking up the spilled water, the blocks, the people. I hate his messes. I know that horses are not this messy. Mama says it is our fate to be left with the mess, but I don't think she likes it any more than I do.

She pays very little attention to me actually. She thinks I just read and I'm pretty sure she doesn't realize about the change. To a horse. She acts as though I'm still a girl. She doesn't observe closely.

Administering herself first aid

The fact is there is a fossil in my hoof.

At school we have a hill that is called Fossilhill because there are a lot of fossils to be found there. Actually the fossils are very easy to find. You just pick up a handful of dirt and you come up with fossils. The trick is to find big fossils. I can always find the biggest fossils of anybody, snails and funny sea snakes and shells of all kinds.

The boys run up and down Fossilhill and don't look where they're going. It's no wonder they don't find many fossils. They come and pull Horse's mane. They scuff through where Horse is digging with her hoof. They sometimes try to capture Horse, since she is perhaps the last mustang and of great value. But mostly they are silly, these boys. They don't make much sense, just a mess.

Today I was trotting on the side of the hill and found the biggest fossil I have ever found in my life, which in horse is I think twelve or maybe twenty-four years old. Then I found more and more fossils and other children came to the hill, even the girlygirls who never look for fossils because they always play games I don't know how to play, House and Shopping and Bad Baby. But they tried to find fossils today and asked me if this was a fossil or that, and they found many, many fossils. And we all had a good time. And when we had found all the fossils we had time to find, our teacher said, Put them in your pockets, children, and if you don't have pockets put them in your socks. And we did, and that's why there is a fossil in my hoof.

Girlygirls vs. *Boyannoys* vs. *Horse*

In my kindergarten there is a girl whose name is Larch. It is a funny name for a girl. It might not be such a funny name for a horse, but Larch isn't a horse because she is in fact the girl leader because she decides what games are going to be played and will let the boys tie her up. And the other girls too. When they tie people up they don't use real rope because our teacher wouldn't allow that. If they tie me up with their pretend rope it doesn't work. They think I just don't want to play, but the truth is I'm a horse and stronger than a girl and can break their girlygirl rope.

It's more fun being a horse. More fun than being a girl too, because they just play Housekeeping Area and none of them really knows yet how to read even though they pretend to. I can tell because they can't get the hard words. So they don't let me play with them. My mother says it's all right because they wish they could enjoy stories themselves and next year they will all read and everything will be all right.

The reading is the real problem between the horse and the girls. I guess. But sometimes they do let me play with them, if they need a victim or a hostage or an offering.

Herself among the others

Horses are I think lucky. They do not seem to have friends, such as people, you know, for they do not seem to need friends. They have enemies—the snakes, the potholes, the cougars, the fancy-booted cowboys who don't know the difference between a canter and a hand gallop. What friends they have are on a very practical basis. Other horses with the same problems.

The wind.

A talk with herself

If I tell her what I am she will not believe me.

If I tell the others what I am they may rope me and tell me to pull their wagon.

If I tell a boy what I am he will invade my loquat house, and maybe it will be good and maybe it will be bad.

If I tell Daddy what I am he will act interested for a minute and then drink some beer and start reading again.

And if I tell Bother he will not understand even the words but will grab my mane and pull it until he has pulled some of it out.

What does it matter? What does it all matter? I will whinny and run away.

Who could blame me? Horses should not be abused, ignored, or made fun of.

Discussing the weather or nothing at all

Just a little while ago, when I needed to go out to race a bit and throw my head in the wind, she stopped me, my dam-mother, and asked me who I thought I was. A girl? A horse? My name? I know what she's thinking. The others at school ask me the same question.

So I said, A girl, because I know that's what I'm supposed to think. One thing I know, not a girlygirl, which would be stupid playing games talking teasing being tied to the junglegym. I won't. Sometimes it's hard not telling her what I really think, what I know. That sometimes I'm a girl, sometimes I'm a horse. When there are girlthings to do, like read, which a horse never does, or go in the car to the stockshow or for ice cream or any of those things, I have to be a girl, but when there are hillsides of grass and forests with lowhanging boughs and secret stables in loquat trees, I am a horse.

Maybe someday there will be no changing back and forth and I will be stuck a horse. Which will be all right with me. Because horses think good easy things, smooth green and windy things, without large people or Bothers or other kids or school, and they have enough grass to trot in forever and wind to throw their manes high to the sky and cool sweet stream water to drink, and clover.

The Baby Picture

My sister Sweetbaby can smile like her middle name is Sugar when she wants, and that smile gets Daddy beside himself, though he'd just as soon never let on. He likes it when she calls him Daddysugar, and where, in a family like this somebody like me, named Sid, fits in, I'm trying to figure out.

"Daddy," I say, "you know perfectly well Sweetbaby took to using lemon juice on that mousy hair of hers back in the seventh grade. Why are you throwing fits over her beauty-shop bills now?"

Daddy hardly ever talks these days, and now, having broken his silence to give me what-for over my little sister's costly grooming, he just sits and smiles at his glass of Jack Daniels. I might suggest what I've been thinking for the last several years, that he'd overdone in the whiskey department, but I know I might just as easily as not get a cuff on the ear if I did. It wouldn't make a speck of difference to Daddy that I am twenty-four going on -five and a woman of more-or-less independent means, by which I mean I've reached the approved station in life for headstrong girls who think college is one of life's necessaries. I teach school with one hand and tend house for Daddy and Sweetbaby with the other, and because of my job at the Consolidated I don't have to ask Daddy for anything anymore, which may be part of the problem. I live at home because at first they needed me, and now Daddy wouldn't have it any other way. He says an apartment wouldn't be respectable, everybody would talk. You'd think a parent would be proud of a child wanting to be independent, but there's no predicting Daddysugar, which is Sweetbaby's name for him, not mine.

Sweetbaby's nineteen and in love, and Daddy would have a fit all over again if he finds out the wrong way about this one. Maybe he already knows or suspects, which might account for his starting in with Jack at two P.M. today instead of four. As for me, I think they figure they've got another spinster on their hands, like my Mama's sorry sister, who isn't really sorry and I love her very dearly, but she's simply petrified. Just the way she was thirty-five years ago when she was a young girl too and fellows would come to call. Pompadour hairdo, little white gloves, leg-makeup left over from The War. While Sweetbaby has always been the fetching one, no doubt about it. Curly hair, used to be golden, and now is again. Her glory, her best feature, Granny always used to say and Gran was always right, or so everyone pretended. Sweetbaby's always had some boy or other in tow, as long as I can remember, and she goes through them like a fox through a henhouse. Last spring it was that wild photographer, David, who wanted her for a model, him and his darkroom. Then it was Leon, the grocery-store stockboy who rode a big Harley till he laid it on top of him one summer afternoon. Discernment never was Sweetbaby's strong suit, and even if she ignores it, I notice they're all mighty anxious to see the inside of our house, drink Daddy's whiskey, and talk to him about his fancy foreign cars, the likes of which this town never saw till Daddy. Cars being the only subject Daddy will talk about to perfect strangers.

"Now you lay off Sweetbaby," Daddy tells me, as I could have guessed he would. "I think her hair's right pretty and so do most other folks." Daddy can more than afford to keep Sweetbaby in peroxide, but he likes to make me pay in hide, just to keep things interesting.

Just then who should stroll through the door but the Queen of Sheba herself, and on her back my new dusty rose cashmere cardigan. She gives me her look-to-kill, but her eyeliner's heavier on the left eye than the right. The Christian, sensible thing to do would be to tell her, let her fix her paint before presenting herself to the world looking half-simple. That's what most folks would want, would look upon it as a favor. Not Sweetbaby. Lord knows, I'd be the one in error, criticizing. You'd think I'd know by now that Sweetbaby couldn't put on eyeliner wrong. Her middle name's Max Factor.

So I will keep a still tongue in my head, and let the eyeliner be Sweetbaby's cross. Those eyes! Since the fourth grade there's been an ongoing battle, Sweetbaby versus the spectacles. Personally I'd not mind one bit having a nice pair of hornrims to hide behind. But I got Daddy's 20-20. And since she got her glasses the year that Mama left, Sweetbaby takes her nearsightedness as just one more personal insult I've deliberately contrived. So last summer in the midst of everything she got herself some contact lenses. Now when she came home from the eye-place all bleary-eyed and squinty, Daddysugar liked to have a fit. He throws plenty of fits about Sweetbaby, but never one to match this. "You look positively ridiculous," he told her then and there, and swore a blue streak at that damn fool doctor. "Take them damn things out of your head this minute and get me my money back, Sweetbaby."

Sweetbaby wasn't about to give up those blue contact lenses that made her eyes match Daddysugar's (her real eyes are light brown), and she started in crying for real. "If you think for one minute, Daddysugar, that I'm going through life with these here wire rims," which she just had to have last spring, when they were the rage, "you've got another think a-coming." And with that Sweetbaby stared Daddy down.

"If you can hold your eyes open to stare your poor old Daddy down like that, Sweetbaby, you can just as well keep them open that way all the time. No more squinty-eye and you can keep those instruments of torture." And that was the end of that, everybody won, and that was how Sweetbaby perfected her look-that-could-kill, which she's using on me at this very minute with regard to that new cashmere I bought out of my second paycheck from the Consolidated School District.

Against my better judgment, I say, "That sweater looks right nice, Sweetbaby. Where'd you get it?"

"You know perfectly well where I got it," she says, without batting an eye. "Are you trying to start trouble, Siddy?"

Well, I had started it. "It looks just like...no, it couldn't possibly be. I got one very like it the other day, down at Himmelblau's. But mine's not even out of the tissue paper."

"Don't be cute," Sweetbaby says, jutting her jaw and showing all her teeth, which are finally straight now, even though she sucked her thumb till she was twelve. And rocked in bed, to boot, humming away.

"I'm glad to see we agree on at least one thing, our taste in sweaters," I say. And Daddy says nothing and smiles at his friend, Jack. Sometimes I think he likes a good fight, as long as he's not in it.

Not batting an eye, Sweetbaby says, "I don't have anything to wear with this skirt." And she turns her back my way.

"And you still don't, Sweetbaby. Now you put that new sweater of mine back where you found it or I'll scratch your buggy eyes out."

"You hear that, Daddy?" Sweetbaby says. "You going to let Siddy get away with threatening me like that? I got an important date this afternoon, Daddy. You know. I told you."

"It's all right, girl," Daddy croons. "Whose sweater is that you got on there, Sweetbaby?"

My sweet baby sister doesn't say a word. She just bursts into those practice-makes-perfect crocodile tears.

"It's all right, honeylamb," Daddy says. "I'll get you your own cashmere sweater. Poor little thing, no job or nothing. I'll get you two, baby. Now don't you cry, darling." And to me, he says, "You ought to be ashamed of yourself, so selfish, Siddy."

"Too big anyway," Sweetbaby says, and all but sticks out her tongue.

Daddysugar's been like this ever since his blue-eyed Mamalove ran off to the other side of town with the Jewish lawyer, Seymour Gold. And that's been ten years and then some. No one in town acted the least surprised when it happened. They mostly sighed and said it had been going on for years, was only a matter of time, Mama and Seymour. People talked all right, but not the way you'd expect. Everyone seemed to think it was kind of romantic, and so all right, what they called "impossible love," which started when they were practically children themselves—when the merchant Gold's son had the fool notion to come to a dance at the Masonic Temple. Mamalove turned out the only girl who'd dance with him. A town this size everybody knows that kind of thing, savors recalling it, with a mighty thin disguise of social outrage.

Of course Mama's exodus took place before the natural gas came in, and if she'd known about that, she'd never in a million years have thrown Daddy over for Seymour. For a time I thought Mama was a very complicated person, doing what she did, but then I realized with Mama things come down to one thing and one thing only. Money. When she up and left, Mamalove thought she was getting rid of a loafing, spoiled ne'er-do-well, our Daddy, who never had to work a day in his life, and taking up with someone who, as she put it to me, had a little fire in his ass. A delicate way with words, Mama has, and Sweetbaby takes after her. Well, Mama and I haven't spoken since she decamped. Daddy's pride and joy can do no wrong, and Daddy thinks she's playing double agent visiting Mamalove's house on the 12th hole of the country club every other Sunday. She gives Daddy to know she's reporting fully on Seymour's every whipstitch, but in fact she just turns the knife in the old wound. Dumb old Daddy, letting Mama have her fool divorce, which was only her way of daring him to do something. "If you try stopping her, she'll come back," I told Daddy, but he told me to mind my own business, Mamalove had already made one spectacle too many. Really he was too hurt to fight back, and then took up with Jack Daniels as his best friend. Seymour and Mamalove tried their level best to clean Daddy out proper. They did a fairly good job. When they were finished all he had left was his granddaddy's old house and some old scrubland, not worth fighting for, back in the hills. That way they could say they'd left him something. As it turned out, they didn't realize *what* they'd left him, for if they had, they'd have left him something else. "Impossible," Daddy said when the gas was struck, and I can just about figure what Mamalove had to say. Poor Daddy with more money than even his granddad, more than Mama ever dreamed, more than Seymour Gold's whole family put together, and Daddy too stubborn to say a word to Mama, even passing each other in the bank every Monday morning, now just sitting, drinking his whiskey and ice, nursing the bitter off-Sunday afternoon and spoiling Sweetbaby rotten. "Radcliffe, no sir," he said to me when I wanted to make plans for college. "Just don't you think for one minute you can fool your own Daddy, Siddy. You and your Mama, I know your kind. I know what you're up to, plotting something, planning on sneaking off to Cambridge, Massachusetts, with that James boy. Don't you forget for one second I went to high school with his old man—his ma, too, for that matter—and I got my gullet full of second-hand Harvard stories twenty-five years ago." Daddy was right, of course; that was what Roger Lee and I had in mind, though I didn't think Mama's situation was quite the same as mine, and I couldn't see what was wrong with the James family or their chemical toilet company. Still don't, though Roger's married to somebody else and moved off to Chicago. So I went to the Normal School, and acted glad of it. Which brings me to Quentin.

"Problem is, Daddysugar," I say with some difficulty, "someone I know has been wanting to meet you."

"Don't you Daddysugar me," he says, humpfs, and sights me over the rim of his Jack Daniels.

"A fellow I teach with at the Township Consolidated High School. Math. Track coach. I think you might just like Quentin." I rush on, trying with all my might to sail through this the way I know Sweetbaby would be able to. Don't let anybody get a word in edgewise, that's her secret. Arrange the holes in the conversation where they can't help but do you good. How I'll ever manage to tell Daddysugar that I guess I'll marry Quentin, I don't know.

"Some other day, Siddy. Sweetbaby's asked her boyfriend by."

"I'm cooking the dinner," I say, "and I've already invited Quentin to eat with us."

"You best ask Sweetbaby if it's all right with her," he says, almost not paying attention. All at once I know that Daddy no more knows who he is, where he is, what he is, than the man in the moon, and it has nothing whatever to do with Jack Daniels. Poor Daddy never did know. Mama saw it, and didn't help one bit.

"Well, who is it you finally snagged?" Sweetbaby says, sneaking up behind me.

"I haven't snagged anybody, Sweetbaby. But maybe he's snagged me."

"Listen to this sass, Daddysugar," Sweetbaby says. "What's his name." Sweetbaby sounds all of a sudden bored.

"Quentin. Quentin Ames is his name. A fellow I teach with."

"But who *is* he?" she asks, meaning something altogether different. Who people were never bothered Sweetbaby before. "Come on," she says, all but tapping her toe, "you know exactly what I mean." She stares at me, those myopic eyes bugging out, trying to do me in with a Sweetbaby whammy.

"Sweetbaby, I got porkchops to stuff and put in the oven, and yams to candy."

"Oh, my ass. Make it dinner for five, then, if your big stud is planning on freeloading a meal." Sweetbaby's never made any effort to be genteel. In fact, I think she believes Daddy likes her dirty mouth, even if he claims not to. She takes that after Mamalove, and Daddy didn't mind it in her. Sweetbaby's past is not exactly pure as the driven snow either, though she made me promise, cross my heart, never to tell Daddy or anyone else what really happened with the Harley-rider—that the real reason we went to St. Louis last summer was not to shop for Sweetbaby's college wardrobe but to get rid of the motorcycle-baby. Then what did Leon do but turn his Hog over on top of himself when he found out what Sweetbaby had gone and done and that she wasn't going to Southern State the way they'd planned, but to some fancy school in Virginia she read about in a horse magazine, where she was scheduled to learn to build jumps and polish flat-saddle tack with the best of them. That school more than had its work cut out, and Sweetbaby refused to go back after Thanksgiving. "Too much horse-shit," she told everybody in town who asked, even the Presbyterian minister, in true Sweetbaby style. Truth of the matter is Sweetbaby never finishes anything, babies, school, you name it. So now, coming on to Christmas, Sweetbaby has herself this new Wilson trotting along behind her, pestering her day and night, barely able to keep his hands to himself, and lowlife Leon, in traction, is out of sight, out of mind.

What's come to Quentin's face more than anything is a dazed look, pure shock. "You're...different from them," he whispers to me when Sweetbaby and Wilson leave the room for a fresh glass of whiskey for Daddy and a few intimacies better left to the imagination. "I mean, she looks...sort of fast, sort of tough," he says, me looking as though it's total news, as though never have I heard the same thing before, though I have, many times. "I guess it's the makeup," he says, then checks himself. "What am I saying? She's your *sister.*" He is flustered, embarrassed and stopped dead in his tracks. Wilson is probably this minute saying how dowdy I am, so I might as well own up.

"It's all right," I tell him. "Most people say the same thing. It must be so." But I hope Daddy hasn't heard him, 'cause Quentin would stand as much chance with Daddy as a snowball in hell if he'd heard him blacken Sweetbaby's name.

"Say, Quentin—that's an odd name!—you know what *Sid* really means?" Sweetbaby says, flouncing back into the room, rousing

Daddy with the ringing cubes in his just-poured glass of whiskey. I look at her to say *shut up,* but she won't look my way. Sweetbaby's never been one to do me any favors; from little on, it's been her or me. She'd just as soon I rot here forever with Daddysugar, doing the job Mama ran out on, so Sweetbaby won't have to be bothered. Sometimes I wonder if they're all in it together.

"It's kind of interesting, actually," old Sweetbaby goes on, earnest as a snake. "Sid really stands for S.D.," she says, and she pauses dramatically, waiting.

"And?" Quentin rises to the bait like some dumb sunfish.

"And—now don't you kill me, Siddygirl," she mocks me with her fake concern, "S.D. stands for Sugar Dumplin'! You see," she says, no thought of letting anybody get a word in edgewise now, "Sid has always had this weight problem." Sweetbaby is all at once cozy, confidential. "I've always been just the opposite. Did Siddy show you her baby picture over yonder on the baby grand? You have to see it for yourself, Quentin. What a scream!"

Quentin squirms like a worm in hot ashes, poor fellow. Take that, Quentin, your baptism by fire. Sweetbaby must have heard us before. "No, ma'am," he says finally, "I haven't seen the picture. You play the piano, Sid?"

"Sure does," chimes in Sweetbaby. "Me, I came along after Mama was all wore out from nagging old Sid to practice, so I can't play a note."

"Just on the radio," says Wilson, his first and last contribution to the conversation.

"Play 'Moonlight Sonata' for the man, Sid, and don't pull that coy act."

It's been three years at least since I've played anything worth mentioning, and Sweetbaby knows it just as well as anyone. "After dinner," I plead off. "It's time to eat now," I say, realizing at last there are some small advantages to being cook in this house.

Now Daddy has stomped out of the room, and out of the house for all I know, and Sweetbaby's smirking up a storm there in the archway to the front hall. "I could have told you he'd blow a gasket," she says. Quentin still looks like he's in shock. Baby sister won't let it lay. "If just for once in your life, Sid, you'd confide in your own sister. If I knew what you wanted to talk to Daddy about tonight, I could've told you not to."

"Who do you think you are, Sweetbaby? When have you ever been anything but a big fat bundle of prohibitions? And when do you think of anybody but yourself? Other people have rights, though you'd never know it, the way you act."

"Your timing is wrong, Siddy, and if you'd just listen to me for a minute instead of running your mouth on I'd tell you Daddysugar and Wilson had a very important talk just this very afternoon. About me and Wilson." With that, she stops cold. Quentin and I look at each other and divine the rest.

I almost can't bear looking at this dear, sweet, unsuspecting man, who no more had a notion of what a nest of spitting vipers he was getting into than the man in the moon. It's all wrong, I think for just a moment, the idea of getting married to Quentin, or anybody else for that matter. Then I look up and see Sweetbaby smiling down on us, our confusion and dismay her day's handiwork, and I swear to god that if Quentin will still have me after this fiasco, I will marry him and leave this place and these people, if it is the last thing I do. Now Sweetbaby is rattling on, as she sometimes does, about how Daddy needs me so, going into all about Mama leaving for Seymour Gold, knowing how that gets to me, and finally about how she's going to do her part tending to Daddysugar by bringing Wilson into the family, since Wilson will see to Daddy's business affairs once he gets through his Business Administration course out at the Junior College. And I know, as well as I can know anything, that though they both will say that I am needed here, it's not that I am needed here, but that someone is. That I would be the least inconvenient solution, and that Sweetbaby has no intention of letting an aging Daddy cramp her style. I take Quentin by the hand to the bench at the baby grand and start to play, not the "Moonlight Sonata" but the Chopin "Polonaise" Sweetbaby despises.

"Well," Sweetbaby says, and she stomps off to find the future's business administrator. What I could tell that man, I think, but then I think again. I doubt there's very much he doesn't already know that he can't guess. They'll make a good pair.

Something for a Rainy Day

Arthur was in the dream from which Hope awoke before there was any light outside, the same dream she'd had before, but today instead of giving in to the washing consciousness that would erase the dream's details increasingly as the day wore on—so that by afternoon the only sensation she would have left would be that of the vague familiarity that it had happened again—she lay, her eyes wide and fixed on the cream-colored ceiling, watching, thinking, listening, remembering, sorting the pieces of yesterday that might have triggered the dream again (for she had read that certain dreams had such causes), and deciding that this once, this particular time, she would remember the dream fully and permanently.

Arthur was in the dream, her only recurrent dream, still. That was probably a good enough reason for Hope usually to try to rub it from conscious memory. Arthur. Brave Arthur, cowardly Arthur, and what might have been. Arthur and Hope, not just Arthur, that was what the dream was really about, she realized. Now her whole leg throbbed, but Dr. White had said to expect pain in the morning, and Hope had come to will it and her broken hip away from conscious thought, as she had done with other things. Out of sight, out of mind. Mother had been a repository of old adages, but now Mother was gone and sometimes Hope had to think long and hard before the appropriate saying would spring up from memory. Two's company, three's a crowd. Monkey see, monkey do. Still water runs deep. God helps those who help themselves. Keep your own counsel. A man's best friend is his dog. You can't teach an old dog new tricks. It was too confusing, there was no consistency in those wisdoms. The familiar sound of them gave Hope some comfort, but what lay beneath the words poked at her, contradictions intruding on quiet memories. Which of Mother's sayings pointed the one true, correct way?

Hope stirred, feeling the dream already evaporating, her eyes tracing the edges of the room's ceiling carefully, focusing her attention on those immediate right angles so that, she hoped, she would not lose those oblique messages. Sent from...she didn't know where. Arthur, somewhere, sending her these dreams? Was it possible? They might just as well be sent from him. No one could really explain dreams, or could prove their explanations. Stop, I won't let you go. Those were the words. She had said them in the dream, those words exactly. That much she had hold of. And Arthur, marvelous in his sailor-suit. God, how awful were the middy-blouses they used to wear in gym class, when she was a girl in school. But how handsome Arthur had been in his, how tall, with his wet hair combed flat except for one big wave that would never mind his efforts and came down far on his forehead right away. His other curls would eventually loosen too, the sides, but always first the heavy lock that came down in front. His almost-black hair was the same color as Hope's had been, so alike that people always remarked. The face she could see as clear as day, as in her dream, but not the total picture. Hope still had the snapshots taken that last Saturday before Arthur left. If she needed to, she could always get those out. It must have been years since she had looked at them, but she always knew exactly where they were: they lay, not fastened in, in the album at the bottom of the drawer of extras, the place where she kept all the extra gloves, scarves, lingerie, stockings, handkerchiefs—whatever Hope had bought on sale or on trips without really needing them, except to need them in the sense that she'd always been told she needed a drawer of extras. Always put something away for a rainy day, and she did. Some of the petticoats from the sixties were much too short to ever wear now, and she regretted having hoarded so carefully those boxes of 60 gauge 15 denier stockings, all toeless, that she might as well give away now. Too late for them. Willful waste makes

Willful want. Or was it, Better safe than sorry? She would not have to look yet at the album; even that much of a face-to-face encounter with Arthur frightened her. Was she being silly, or was there something dangerous in seeing him, if just in those photographs, especially so soon after this dream emanation. The fates couldn't be trusted. The doorbell might ring. It might be Arthur in person. She would just die.

I won't let you go, Arthur, the dream Hope had said, had said it as if she truly meant it. Dream Arthur was ready to leave, Arthur sweating only slightly, a miracle of calm in the sticky July heat and his heavy Navy uniform. He had put his gob-hat on Hope's shiny dutch bob and then kissed her, and then someone had snapped one of the pictures, Arthur looking straight ahead, squinting a smile into the sun (always have subjects stand facing the sun, the instructions read), somewhat but not completely happy, and Hope, her shoulders thrown forward, her dark head thrown back, nestled swanlike in the surrounding arm of Arthur, raising her face to his, looking at him, not the trees or the beautiful summer sky or the camera, only at him. Did the ring show in that picture? She could remember, if she could think about it for a minute. Yes, they were standing in such a way (he on her right, his left arm around her, she with her right arm around behind his waist, yes, her left hand with the star ruby resting lightly, proprietorially, on Arthur's chest) that his ring would show. Definitely, yes she remembered. Arthur had given her the ring in June. The picture was the last of July.

And again it was July, and the accident, when she shattered her hip, had happened the previous one. Hope's birthday was in July, the fifteenth. Arthur had gone away in July, though that was practically ancient history. 1942. Thirty-eight years ago. She had just turned nineteen, and Arthur was twenty-two. Her hip, her whole leg hurt like hell. But if she took a pill for the pain, the dream would rush off into that place where dreams came from, and she wanted, for the moment, for the dream to stay.

What would Arthur, who used to joke endlessly about being a Leg Man, think of her now? His jokes made her think of her long slim legs as an asset, not toothpicks. Every afternoon after school, she would lie out tanning in the sun on the hill in back of the house on Garden Street. She might have quit teachers' college, and then where would she be? You'll bake your brains, studying in the sun, everyone told her. But Hope always took the sun well. Her younger sister Peggy was just the opposite, blonde hair, skin like cream. Peggy's thick hair always took days to dry then, though now it was short and fluffy. Peggy always said the sun was her enemy, it would make her old before her time, that her skin was delicate, and it was. Hope's sister took after the Southern aristocratic side of the family, like a treasured heirloom lace doily. She was cultivated, refined in ways that Hope never was or ever tried to be, and never would Peggy be caught looking adoringly into the face of some smiling sailor, least of all on film, for all posterity. Peggy was all the best things, all dove grey and ecru lace, black silk and cluny and dimity. Yet even after all these years of differences, they still lived in the same house, taught at the same school, took part in the same conversations about the same people. Peggy didn't think Hope's clothes were in the best of taste, since they were mostly strong colors, gay prints, daring cuts. And always, until the accident, she wore the kind of shoe that Arthur liked, not the pumps Peggy recommended; Hope wore sandals, summer and winter, even though there came a time when the styles were such that they had to be made especially for her on her own I. Miller last.

This goddamn hip, Hope thought. She would have to get out of bed for a pain pill after all, and the dream would be gone. I won't let you go, she had said to Arthur, and she had meant it, this time. Not that she wouldn't let him go off to war: it was clear he had to. There had been no denying your country in that war, no weirdos or hippies, no shirkers like some of the kids she'd had in her very classes, no sudden blossoming of conscientious objectors. Back then one might as well die as be a CO—no one she knew of in town, with the exception of Edward Wiebel, who would have failed the mental anyway, had done such a thing. No, Arthur's duty had been clear—she knew it, Arthur knew it. The trouble had been then, and now, that Hope's duty had not, no matter how clear everything seemed through the haze of the dream. When the dream Hope said "I won't let you go," she meant yes, she would indeed marry him, then and there. Though that wasn't how it had happened.

How easy it had been for Arthur, with his piece of paper from the government telling exactly what he had to do. Arthur had a war to fight. Step by step his course had been laid out for him, and Arthur didn't really have to think, except in an incidental way, about Hope. That hadn't seemed to take much deciding either. "Inexorable," that's what Arthur said about them, their being together, and that was largely how it had been, once the Mason boy up the street brought

Arthur home with him from Great Lakes that first Christmas. But Hope's duty? She couldn't make heads or tails of it, or of anything. Everything seemed to be speeding past her, though the times between Arthur's furloughs would drag. It did seem that they both knew what things were moving toward, that they both wanted it. But Hope was afraid, knowing that very soon, in a few months, Arthur would be gone. And there was every chance that once he was gone, he would be gone for good.

Marry me, Arthur said, but marry me now. His desperation frightened Hope; she hadn't understood it or expected it. Now. Now, before he shipped out. A lot of servicemen had said the same thing. A lot of people were getting married, quickly. He was headed for the Pacific, she knew it, though he couldn't exactly say so. Right now, July 1942. He got a three-day pass for Decoration Day and hitched a ride most of the way down Route 66 from Great Lakes. A nice old farmer from Carlinville, he said, and then, on the front porch on Garden Street, he gave her the ring from C.D. Peacock's. It was a star ruby, like no ring she had ever seen before, and certainly not like any ordinary engagement ring. Often, later, she wondered if Arthur had known how it would end. The ring took Hope by surprise, there on the porch swing, the two of them drinking iced tea to cool off after Arthur had arrived. The ruby, its star lurking like a secret in its heart, was set in an antique filigree circle. He'd just guessed at the size, and when he saw the star he knew it was the right ring for them because the stars at night would make him feel close to her, after he had to go off to war. His orders were definite now. His folks could come from Iowa, so if she would set the day, maybe his family could make travel arrangements. Or if Hope really didn't want a fuss, war-time and all, they would understand, it would be perfectly all right with him, they would just go down to the County Court House, or if she wanted to go away someplace, if she thought that was more romantic or just if that was what she preferred, anything, he would understand, whatever she said would be perfectly all right with him, he knew it wouldn't upset his parents, though he knew they'd like her immediately and she'd like them too, and he wanted them to meet her very soon, maybe later this summer if they didn't come for the wedding, but they'd always said they'd wanted a daughter, with their three sons, and Arthur couldn't imagine them wanting one any different from Hope, and she would say yes, wouldn't she. Please, Hope, please. Now.

She wanted to. She imagined the press of his body on hers alone in her bed, she imagined his kisses going toward the ear where they became I love you. She knew the only answer she could give was yes, though she thought, for the sake of form, she ought to say she wanted to sleep on it. After breakfast the next morning, she mentioned it to Mother, that she'd stay here, if it was all right, and finish her degree so she could teach. But her mother let it slip to one of her married sisters, who was shocked, and that sister told another married sister, then a cousin, and before Hope knew it there were a thousand words and a thousand ideas, and none of them did she recognize as hers. She shut herself in her room. She cried. No matter what they said, Arthur wasn't trying to take advantage of her, of the situation. How could they?

What did they know of Arthur, and what of Hope? What did Peggy really know, with all her gentility and poise, her concerts and the right people? Did Mother really know how she felt, or did her other sisters, the complacent married ones, their husbands too old or too weak or in some vital industry, safe from the war, nothing whatever to lose. What did any of them know about Hope and Arthur and the war? Hope's sister Darcy left right away to consult with the Reader, and that was why Hope stormed out of the room and told them all to go straight to hell, every last one of them, and let her make up her own mind. Didn't they care whether she was happy or not? What did they care about? Why should they be bothering with her decision, and what was there to decide? And dragging that Reader into all this was the last straw. Have you had any dreams, Mother? her sisters asked. Letty believed that their mother had the gift, and if their mother had owned up to having had any dream on the subject, that would have ended the matter then and there. Well, did you Mother? Peggy asked, when their mother did not respond. Mother finally said that she had not, and moreover she didn't put any stock in such things, that all that foolishness was their idea. She thought people did what they had to do, and she wasn't going to say any more about it. It was Hope's decision, and Arthur's, and everyone should just let them be.

But the Reader would know something, Darcy insisted, and didn't Hope think so too? Hope didn't really like to think about that Reader at all. She'd gone along a few times to her Parlor with Darcy, who thought her husband was cheating on her. The Reader's name was Mrs. Fellowes, and fortunately she lived in the next town—it wouldn't have done to go to her if she lived right here. Mrs. Fellowes gave Hope the creeps, but Darcy never liked to go anyplace by herself, and as long as Hope could remember, she never had. Keep the home fires burning, Mrs. Fellowes advised Darcy, and on the way home she had bought a new nightgown. Arthur was another kind of problem; it wasn't a question anymore of stopping by Gold's Department Store for something frilly. Darcy was positive Hope's situation would be clear as day once she talked to Mrs. Fellowes. I'm not going to your stupid witch, she told Darcy. Leave her be, Mother said, but Darcy had already picked up her black patent shoulder bag and car keys (her husband was the vital industry one, and had all the gas he wanted) —and she was halfway out the door. Darcy, you shouldn't meddle where you're not wanted, their mother said. I'm a married woman, Mother, a grown woman, she said, and I don't take orders from you any longer. And she left.

Shortly after noon she was back. They all heard her whip the Chrysler onto the chat driveway and churn up the hill, and by the time the handbrake was set, Hope's sisters were on the back porch. I don't want any part of this, their mother said, but she came out too, just to listen. Who ever heard tell of such a thing, fortune tellers? she scolded. By the time Darcy got to the back steps, they all appeared to have been casually passing the time of a summer's day, everyone with sweet iced tea. Hope stayed in her room, but the windows were open, and everyone on the back porch took pains to speak distinctly enough to let her hear. Mrs. Fellowes had advised Darcy on any number of real or potential troubles, but yes, to get to the matter at hand, she did have something to say about Arthur. She will never see him again, Mrs. Fellowes said, once he leaves.

The Reader didn't say: Arthur will go down in the Pacific with his ship.

She didn't say: Arthur will be killed in a train wreck on the way to the West Coast, or in a brawl in a brothel in Mindanao, or crossing the street in Seattle, or by sheer cowardly fright during a Kamikazi raid.

Once he leaves, she said, she will never see him again. And although Mrs. Fellowes turned out to be dead wrong about Darcy's husband, and then about Letty's death, which was ruled a suicide, and about

Peggy's awful arthritis and about the economy and about a thousand other smaller forgotten things she had told Hope in the years since, she was not wrong in the least about Arthur. Damn that woman.

So now Hope held the dream, palpable as the glowing star hidden away in the drawer of extras, just as available, should she choose to get it out and look at it. The dream's clarity was oddly complete and detailed, and Hope could hear the dream's voice, a voice like the kind on old radio shows like Lux Presents Hollywood, a kindly narrator who would explain significances to listeners who could not draw conclusions for themselves. Hope took the wrong turn, the voice said. Hope didn't listen to herself. She stroked the empty finger on her left hand and thought, No. I will not let you go. Now I understand the price of caution, now I don't think Arthur is selfish or foolish, the way everyone said.

But what if, somehow, Mrs. Fellowes did know something? What if Hope had married Arthur, and the Reader turned out to be right? What if, by marrying him, Hope had sealed Arthur's fate? No one mentioned that. How would she feel had she taken the selfish step that doomed this man she loved? She didn't believe in readers. They dealt in lies and calculated guesses. But still, she wondered. And she still wondered.

Arthur, where are you now? It was time to get up—she needed a pill for the pain. She had promised Dr. White: only when the pain became unbearable. Arthur hadn't died, whether it was because she didn't marry him or not, and to her knowledge (though her knowledge was a bit sketchy) had not died yet. The last she heard, he had taken over his father's bank in Cedar Falls. Lovely wife, she heard. Three kids. He would be sixty. Thirty-eight years had passed between, almost twice as many as they had even lived when all this happened, and did he remember, too? Exactly how it had happened, Hope didn't want to know, just that a girl from Cedar Falls started writing her old beau who was far away in the war and more lonely than anyone could have guessed. Hope, for whatever reason, had denied him. And Hope hadn't even done what she had really wanted to, or could explain to Arthur. She had let everyone down, Arthur and herself, or so it seemed from the outside. Perhaps she got what everyone thought she had coming, thirty years of high-school French and now this.

She'd had the same dream last year, around her birthday, on the fifteenth, which would have been a nice day to get married, Arthur had said. The birthday must have triggered the dream, another year and more alone than ever. The day always made her think of the wedding that didn't take place, and why, of the letters she'd gotten from him from overseas, still safe in the album in the drawer of extras, and of the letters that finally came at the end, the ones she had to burn or they'd burn her hands, holding them. All day, every year, she'd think. And about Mrs. Fellowes, about Darcy and her divorce and what it did to the family, about Letty, poor gentle weak Letty and the puzzle of her death, about Peggy, who had recently taken up with the faith-healers for her arthritis, about her mother telling her it was her decision. Then Hope, coming from the shower in a cloud of Shalimar and Cuba Libres, shattered her hip, last birthday. A freak fall, the doctor said; he'd never seen anything like it. A safe thing to say; are any two things ever the same? No possible way the hip could be repaired completely, no guarantee she'd ever be able to walk, at least unaided. Pins and plates and god only knew what all. Surgeries and months of therapy. She knew, when it finally looked as though she should be able to get around, that she would never be the same again. Never. One day a man came to her in the hospital, bringing a catalog of undesirables and taking measurements for the doctor's prescription shoes—no sandals. Just one platform, a Frankenstein shoe that broke her heart to see it. Last spring, last spring, Hope in a dream was dancing at the Casa Loma in St. Louis, Guy Lombardo and his Royal Canadians, and strong, tall Arthur, in his uniform, holding her tight, but they were both their ages now. Why had Hope thought she could simply be inert, and all the right things would happen, or that somehow things would turn out all right. No, she didn't want to think about it any more, didn't want the dream any more, and got up, shook out two pills for the real pain in her hip and two for the other kind of pain and hobbled (since getting the circulation going past that hip in the morning was pure hell) to the kitchen for something to wash it all down.

A Wild Lens

Corey Adams is a wrestler, though it doesn't make sense. All the other boys on the wrestling team are such ratty types. Hollywoods and all. Tattoos and all. D.A.'s and silver belts a half an inch wide and pink shirts with metallic threads running through them, worn with the collar turned up. Motorcycle boots, motorcycle jackets. Corey Adams is going to Harvard, he says.

Corey Adams sits in front of me in World History II. Last semester I sat in front of Ricky Harriman, and had a crush on him. Ricky Harriman, it turned out, was not too bright. Ricky Harriman sat behind me because he knew he could get the right answers off my paper. Very foolish of me. Besides Ricky Harriman is of a questionable family. His father is supposed to own all the jukeboxes in town. People say he owns all the slots, too, but I never see any slot machines anyplace, which probably only means I don't go to the right places to see slot machines. Everybody says Ricky Harriman's father is mixed up with The Mob, which is something they always sort of whisper, but I guess all this is what makes Ricky unsavory. Ricky is, besides not being bright, somewhat on the uncouth side, I have learned. He reportedly pulls at the seat of his pants, and all the boys call him Itchy-Ritchy. Ricky has a Rick Nelson complex. He is cultivating a tendril to appear from nowhere in his long crew cut, and he spends many hours with his face in an approximation of the one-side-up half-smile that Rick Nelson has developed to display one of his incisors. For a while it was very appealing, and Ricky Harriman chewed Dentyne. When I would turn around to say something, he would blast me with all that cinnamon. It was something, for a while.

Ricky Harriman took me to a dance once, even. It was not much fun, finally, because all the boys sat around the table playing pyromaniac with the crepe paper decorations, trying to impress and scare all the girls, who had every right to be scared because they all had dresses with lots of tulle ruffles and overskirts. Tulle is a terrible fabric. It itches, and you can't blame the boys for being slow to dance with something that feels like a porcupine. But the dance was the beginning of the end for Ricky Harriman. Not only did he become totally absorbed in his little bonfire, but I spent a lot of the evening with the growing suspicion that it would be much more fun being there with Corey Adams, even if he was on the wrestling team. Corey Adams would probably take his date by the country club afterwards to see what the crowd was doing. The stigmatized gangster child Ricky Harriman, it turned out, took me to a dingy pizza parlor before trying his own kind of wrestling in the back seat, all the while maintaining the Ricky Nelson lip lift. This Ricky was not an original. Not the genuine item. Ricky was not too bright, and it was painful having to play little girl to a boy I knew I was smarter than. No, worse than that, it was ultimately depressing, and I knew when the semester changed, where I would sit in World History II.

So what are *you* doing in town, he asked me. I didn't know how to tell him without being cruel, or was it sheer egotism to think he would be hurt knowing I was here to visit a wonderful wild painter who made him look fifty-five years old. So I said, visiting friends. Well, he said, what are you doing this evening. Things began to run together.

This friend I am here to see is, as I said, a painter. He paints great somber geometric textural things that would be Feiningeresque if the colors had more joy and if he wouldn't fiddle with the surface so much. This friend rides a motorcycle, a huge Harley, that will never start. I have watched this friend all summer long in Vermont jumping up and down on his Harley's starting lever trying to get the thing to start. Black bastard, he would call the machine, and laugh. He was an Aryan type and enjoyed making such comments. Half-Swede, half-Lithuanian. Hugely tall. Somehow dangerous and always delighted when others found him unpredictable. About to have some of his paintings in a show, a real professional show. It upsets me because they are abysmally dull paintings trying to be cerebral. Now that I have finally come to Boston to see him, it seems like a bad mistake. I don't know how to react to the paintings, to him, to his friends. We wander around and around the Isabella Stewart Gardner Museum and the baroque music floats up from the courtyard. The music and the place don't make sense to me and I cannot make the kind of knowledgeable snobby putdown remark that I know would please him. I don't know what to say about carved doors and ikons, about gold and vermeil and gilt. They are not articles of my faith. I cannot reconcile the Purcell I hear now with the black bastard Harley-Davidson that will never start. The snow begins and I don't know what to say on the phone to Corey Adams. I can't say all this. He is waiting. Something simple, sweet, coquettish, nothing brooding, nothing sad.

I'm at the Parker House. Won't you come over and we can have a drink and talk.

Corey Adams' cousin is going to VMI. Corey Adams' cousin has been a central figure in my mythology since I first witnessed him in Miss Smith's kindergarten. His father, a VMI man himself, is a blond southern gentleman, thin of face, long of blond hair, soft of manner toward ladies, gentle of voice, and supposedly related to the Virginia Lees. At the end of the kindergarten year, Corey Adams' cousin disappeared; his military father was shipped and the family must have followed. Ten years later they moved back. Corey Adams' family is the kind that always moves back. At the time I didn't know Corey Adams' cousin was Corey Adams' cousin because I didn't know Corey Adams. Everything became more difficult after that. Corey Adams' mother's cousin's half-sister's daughter's cousin was, it turns out, my best friend. Sylvia was a difficult girl but talented in many ways. Now she has lots of children, but then she ran the student council and she was always at the center of every play the school put on, starting with one when we were freshmen. Sylvia was a coy coed and I was the villainess, an old maid aunt. Sylvia was tiny and blonde and so transparent you could almost see her skull.

You can't mean it, my cousin says to me. I do mean it, I say to him. You can't like *him*, my cousin says, he likes somebody else. Yeah, who, I say to him. Judy Anderson, that's who, he says to me. And Judy Anderson's best friend is your old horse tooth, right, I say to him. Don't you talk that way about her, he says to me. Don't you dare, he says.

We kick the double winged maple seed off the sidewalk before us.

Maybe if he didn't look so much like James Dean it would never have happened, never have turned out this lousy way. I'm not talking now about Corey Adams, who is as far from James Dean as you can get, or about his cousin, the boy who will follow all family traditions without so much as flinching and go to VMI and then be a Rhodes because he's perfect in every way and who is really not a bad substitute for James Dean, or about my nosey cousin who tries to run my life in subtle ways but only bores me with symbolic talk about his black mollies and his angel fish and his beta fish and his siamese fighting fish and his neon tetras, his prides and joys. I know that one day all the fighting fish will kill each other off, the neon colors will fail, the angel fish will fall from grace, the black mollies turn from shadow to transparence. The mudcats at the bottom will be sucked into the mud below, the waving green vines will fill the water, and my cousin will become a promising young vascular surgeon. No, I am talking about the boy who happens to be first-string quarterback.

He is a discipline problem for the teachers. He steals themes from the World Book. He pinches girls' fannies in the halls. He gives teachers the finger with astonishingly poor timing for a quarterback. He knows he looks like James Dean. He would have a Porsche if he could afford one. As it is, no one knows how he affords the '49 Ford coupe, primed. Skirts. Hollywoods. Slight chop. He has been carrying the cigarette behind his ear for two years now. He wears blue jeans and undershirts to school. There are many Natalie Woods.

He likes to drink. That's the problem, the big problem. There is only one game a year that means anything around here, and it takes place on Thanksgiving. The rivalry goes back thirty years. To our parents. The whole school goes wild the day before. The town gets rabid. He got drunk.

The game was a disaster. James Dean got a tattoo. James Dean found a stretch of new highway, the one through German Hollow, where the bridge wasn't finished. It was a big bridge. The concrete posts were there, and the road went up to the edge of the hollow. James Dean jumped the hollow, clear into eternity.

Girls wept for days. Boys wore glum straight-across mouths, they were strong.

Corey Adams' palms are sweating. He is a big boy, though not extremely tall. Rather heavy, I guess you'd say. Probably right for wrestling. He's the center. He passed the ball to James Dean with these very sweaty palms, even though Corey Adams was only a sophomore and James Dean was a senior.

According to the yearbook wrestling picture of James Dean, he weighed a mere 145. His father goes from mine to mine, lasting only until the bottom foreman finds him drunk at the end of a working. James Dean was always picking on something bigger than his own size, something too big for him to handle.

I resolve to pick on someone my own size. I have called the painter in Boston because he is the only one I cannot see straight through, and asked him if he would like me to come and visit him.

Money is no object. The family is willing to send me if it will make me happy. What's an airplane ticket, a hotel bill. The real question is what is happy.

The painter has forsaken the black Harley for a blue Studebaker Land Cruiser. It was the one he wrecked last year, and I am extremely nervous about riding in it. The painter has a jagged red scar across his forehead. I imagine the car is imperfectly repaired and that a wheel may come off at any moment, while we are speeding back to the hotel from visiting friends of the painter's in Byfield. They teach English or history to the sons of talk-show personalities, in a boarding school. They do not seem to have the words to communicate with me, or I with them, and it is all very unreal. I spend the evening wondering what kind of scotch these people are trying to kill me with (it is unbelievably rough) and worrying about my skirt creeping up (it is short) and wondering why the painter wanted to subject me to these dull people who are so impressed with their students' parents. They, however, are probably wondering much the same about me.

The words. I can't remember the words.

They talk about people I don't know, about painters whose work I have never seen, about writers whose poetry is so avant garde only they know of it. They seem to be extremely rude, but the truth of the matter is they are only extremely caught up in proving to themselves that they are in fact brilliant. Their manner puts me in an ungenerous frame of mind. The apartment is sparsely furnished, cheap furniture. The liquor is practically undrinkable. I am beginning to wonder if I like this painter after all, whether it matters that I cannot see straight through him or if I would like what I would see if I could. It is possible that he shows me all this to make me wonder these things. I tell myself that it's not really like that. The painter is in over his head. But if he is, it is because he poses, he wants to be something he is not. His family on a farm in Iowa cannot know him like this. He speaks of them only when I ask, and only opens up somewhat about his brother. A younger brother, and he calls him a blond and naked angel, and he smiles, and I smile; I am with you in Rockland, I say to him. And I think there is some hope, for I have remembered words.

But the real words I cannot remember.

Aunt Justina. Justice personified. The witchy old sister, the professor's old maid sister. The part in a play I had forgotten having a part in. The part in a play the name of which I cannot remember. My life on the boards wasn't much. Not pretty, but a good carrying voice. A villainess? Possibly. The cast went up and I was wishing I hadn't gotten a part after all. The play director is the school bully. She is in fact Justina, but she has cast me as Justina. She is squat and fat and has a beard. She has lately been married, at last, and speaks lovingly to her classes in solid geometry and calculus of her Herman. She is happy. Herman comes to all the evening rehearsals with her. Herman looks recently escaped from a doting family, and happy to be with the play director. They are a happy couple.

Justina! What on earth are you doing. The camera. The bookcase. Good lord, girl, don't you know your lines. Pick it up, girl, pick it up.

The lines. The words. I can't remember. "Why, professor, what a long tail you have." Is that it? No. It couldn't be. The lines. The words.

Now, about costumes. The costume committee is nonexistent, as you know. You'll have to find your own things. Now girls—something cute, pert, coed-ish. Sweaters. Not too tight, not too loose. Something like that would be fine, Sylvia. And professor, a conservative suit, and do you have a grandfather or someone to borrow a hideous old tie from. As dull as you can find. Now Justina, you must look like an old maid. Something somber, a dark sheer with a little figure in it, loose, baggy. I wish your hair were a little longer—well, by the time we go on we'll be able to get it in some kind of knot. Just don't cut it—that includes everybody. Nothing worse than a new haircut on stage. Justina, get some oxfords with heels. Some cotton hose. Herman, are you ready, love?

The director with the beard takes her husband and goes off into the October night, scuffing through the early cottonwood leaves that have piled themselves against the auditorium door. The coeds are going to the Mill to have a coke. They are joking with the professor. Yes, he'd like to go too. They have an afterthought. Would I like to join them. Yes I would. No I wouldn't. James Dean. There will be loud noise at the Mill, no Beethoven sonatas, not even any Brahms rhapsodies, certainly not one of the Chopin concertos. There will be the racketeer's jukeboxes and jokes. James Dean. There will be general hilarity, of which I will not be a part because I never go to the Mill after school, much less at night. There will be shorthand notebooks crammed into American History, Algebra I, II, and V, Civics, Biology, General Business. James Dean. Possibly there will be people getting buzzes from coke and aspirin, or trying to. Or saying they are. Necking in the back booths. Carving on the tables. Peeling in and out of the parking lot. James Dean. Hold yourself above these people, my family says to me. My family, with the addition to the city named after them, with the mines that people fall asleep drunk in and where men lose only legs if they are lucky trying to couple coal cars, with their cars, their big houses and big trees, their bank directorships, their growing troubles with the unions. Hold yourself above these people. It is the posture of a lifetime.

I would like very much to go to the Mill, but it is too much to learn, too much to unlearn. I have fallen behind in my study of life at the Mill. It is an insurmountable task, and to actually go there, just once even, would amount to a deception beyond the lie about what time rehearsal got over. They might come looking and see the long Gothic auditorium, brick with its sandstone trinity of arches, and they would know I was somewhere else. There could be a terrible scene. There have been scenes before.

Another time, maybe, I tell them, and fall even further behind. I plow through the loud leaves as Mr. Richards, the auditorium janitor, says, "Goodnight, Justina," and turns off the work light.

Where are they, faces straining against the east sun? They are the census roll for a German village. Dahm. Yocks. Wolz. Pflanz. Gross. Bretsch. Baum. Krupp. Rhein. Fink. Birnsteihl. Etling. Burkhart. Schaller. Neumeyer. Mueller. Brecknitz. Pfingsten. Eckert. Voelkel. Finklein. Stenger. Kuenkler. Gundlach. Fellner. Mager. Kaiser. Lindhorst. Rauschkolb. Klugge. Cruikshank. Muskopf. Kniepkamp. Ihlanfeldt. Sauerwein. Lindemann. Dintleman. Eilering. Rosenberg. Schaumleffel.

What sun, no sun, some sun blinds their eyes now? What innocent yearbook sun squinted their eyes then? What quiet sun sets on them, where are they spread, quiet against the earth, ankles crossed, sipping a coke or beer or anything, in the backyard of America, a Sony blaring the top 40, a different top 40, Ed Bonner gone now, no Ed Bonner and the Bunny on WIL, the Wild Child gone into the nowhere air, melted like ice in a summer drink, all the names gone, sitting on twenty pieces of spun polypropylene webbing stretched from aluminum tube to aluminum tube, sagging with the weight of football muscles gone soft, turned to beer bloat, of the cheerleaders' cheers gone sour with yesterday's diapers. Does it matter that the sun blinded you then as now?

The mail brings an invitation. The artist is having a one-man show, his first, in Newburyport in somebody or other's gallery. There is to be a gala reception, I gather. The people who foist off bad scotch will be there, I know. The invitation is in the form of a large postal card, and the picture is a black and white reproduction of one of the more important works to be shown. It doesn't fare too well in black and white. I had not been aware that there was so little variety in value in his work. The subject, which the reverse says is "Yachts at Ogunquit," is almost impossible to make out. About all there is for me is a terse geometry that apparently was an early part of the painting. I am not sure whether "Yachts at Ogunquit" is something I saw in his studio or whether it is just that I dream or imagine I have seen the painting or whether all his paintings are so alike that I cannot tell the difference or whether that's a bad thing after all because it would give cohesion to his work or whether it matters whatever way it is. There are plenty of masters who don't do so well in black and white. I call the painter. Long distance. How wonderful, I tell him. Aren't you just thrilled that you're having your own show, I ask him. Yes, I suppose so, he says, for he never wants to lose his Nordic image. I think it's grand, I say, not sure why. Would you be coming, he asks. No, I say, I don't think it's possible. Well, he says, it's not much, really. It's a very small gallery, he says. But your own show, I say, and you should be proud. Well, he says. Well, I say. You remember the owner of the gallery, he says. I do, I ask. Yes, we visited them when you were here, he says. Oh, I say.

Well, it's very nice of her to give you a show, I say. It all begins to look very different from that summer in Vermont when he jumped up and down on the Harley; it begins to look like the Gardner Museum and dull conversation and music that makes no sense but is an excellent conversation point. These things cannot be said. The tone of his voice is strange. He identifies with lots of great painters. He is not an original, either, and originality means something here. He talks briefly, again, about his auto wreck and Jackson Pollock. I want this talking to end. Have a good show, I say. Have a good show, he says and laughs. I put the phone down and never hear his voice again.

For god's sake, it's the middle of winter, he says. You can't have a John Collins.

That's what you think, I tell him.

Well, all right, he says, expelling lots of air, sighing so everyone around can hear. I suppose he is exasperated, embarrassed.

Don't worry, I tell him, trying to make it sound like a joke. Your cool friends from Harvard won't see you here. I doubt if they frequent such square establishments as this.

You're quite right, you know, he says. I do not like the phoney Up East inflections his voice has taken on. I would like to remind him right here and now that southern Illinoisians do not talk like that.

They don't have soft a's and they don't talk in quites and rathers and terriblys and smashings and bloodys. They don't lose their r's. He has been here four years. Who knows what happens to a person in four years.

And so you think you'll go on to the business school next year, I ask.

Right-o, if they'll have me, he says, fiddling with the crease of his trousers. The waiter comes. Yes, waiter, he says. A, and here he pauses and then says as if he can't believe he's really saying it, *John Collins,* and he raises his eyebrows and looks at me. And a double Gibson for me, than-*cue.*

Corey Adams' highschool muscles were a flash in the pan. His face is fatter and his acne hasn't given up yet, his hands somewhat ham-like. He tells me he swims regularly, still. I doubt it, but that's what he says. The difference, Corey Adams, is that I know a John Collins is supposed to be a summer drink and I don't care. You do.

Because Corey Adams has said he swims regularly, I pull apart the orange slice and remember seeing him sometimes at the pool at the club, where he swims frantically and full steam for the wall of the pool and then does a racing turn, except most of the time Corey Adams gets stuck half-way around and misses the wall and doesn't get himself pushed off right. Then he comes up and looks around and sputters in the water. Consarn, he says, in his best Ivy manner. And all the provincials are impressed with his gentlemanly self-control, if not with his racing turn. Similarly, we are to be impressed with his starts. He will stand, sometimes for ten minutes or more, with his toes clinging to the edge of the pool, his eyes far away. He will shake one arm violently, from the shoulder, from the elbow, from the wrist. Then the other arm. Then both arms. Then the legs. Then he will jump up and down and then bend over and shake his head with great violence. Then he will again grip the edge of the pool. His eyes grow glassy with the roar of the meet, his ears listen for "Swimmers, to your marks." There, it is heard. There, the gun. There, the flinging of the arms from their birdlike backwardness, forward, forward, forward, out and out and out, flat over the water, out out out, and the stinging stinging hurt against the thighs and chest and two butterflies and Corey Adams is through.

Dean is gone, married to the stonecutter's daughter who chewed gum and looked like Natalie Wood, all dark brown eyes and precocious figure, the girl who brought True Romance to eighth-grade science class and then was gone, wore felt skirts with telephones and poodles and hotrods appliqued on them, a dog collar around the outside of her triple roll socks, a quarter in her penny loafers, red lipstick, and goldbricking in PE to read the song lyric magazines, sha-na-na and houn' dawg and graduation day and green door and splish splash and mabelline and don't talk back.

Corey Adams, you are impossible if you think I'm going to ride all over Cambridge on the back of a Vespa. He looks at me, still exasperated. No, he says, just to the parking lot. The car's there, he says, and it's only about a mile. Look, Corey, I say, the streets are wet, can't you see that. I am not about to ruin this perfectly good coat, Corey Adams, by having all the slop on the Cambridge streets spattered all over me. Corey Adams' problem is that this is Harvard and it's plebeian to care about things like a nice coat, whereas it's important not to drink John Collinses in the dead of winter. Sorry, Corey, it's the only nice coat I happen to have at the moment and I do care, and you're a phoney if you pretend you don't because being where you are is the ultimate of caring. You couldn't care more. About what seem to me to be the wrong things. Next year you will be in the business school and you will care more than ever, but you always have to be careful not to care, and show it, about things you shouldn't care about. That sounds difficult to me, but you will succeed, I am sure. The distinctions are clean and invariable. Do you ever worry about James Dean, who caused your hands to sweat? I think you must have by now forgotten the whole mythic place where you heard the crowds roar as you kicked the ball off the tee, where you knew the wet grunting of the wrestling matches, the cottonwood drifts, the rain in fall the rain in spring the flooding of the one creek and the rush the rush the always rush, the danger of hayrides, the music, the music, the Zoroastrian religion, the light, the light. It is all distilled: imaginary swimming meets and mildewed wicker chairs. The last slice of the pie. The wild lens spins: the VMI man builds new soldiers at West Point.

The wild lens spins.

The maybe Natalie Wood marries the maybe James Dean. Natalie Wood in real life did not marry James Dean. In real life this Natalie Wood may not have married James Dean. It is the work of the wild lens.

I look sometimes in big cities for Natalie's face outside burlesque houses.

The wild lens spins.

And the last thing I want to remember is this: Natalie Wood took James Dean's class ring and wound it with thread thread thread and painted the thread with airplane gunk to a shiney shiney black to match his jacket, her hair, his mood, her look, and every weekend of the world ripped the thread and gunk and all off and changed it then to red and then to blue and then all sparkles, and the last was golden.

The Principal Parts of **to dance**

Like bee stings, painful hives of fear dot my breast. My hands are cold, his hands are sweaty. Someone tells me cold hand, warm heart, and I wonder about the reverse, and only years later learn that the human male breaks into sweat at a lower body temperature than the female. For now twenty blowing strumming percussing swaying men dressed in sky-blue blazers sit behind bedazzling miniature forts, swirled and glittered *LA*'s sparkling on every one. Straplessness in this world is de rigueur. My black velvet bodice is boned securely as a summer's swimming suit, so why have the hives come? There will be no scenes from the *National Geographic* tonight, and the *LA*'s fill the Elks' with Deep Purple. I look around at the others in their strapless gowns and they have hives too as they learn what it is to dance.

He more or less holds my hand, limply, and braces my back with the other.

We make a box, and another, and another.

We are dancing.

No matter what the tempo, what the rhythm, what the music, we box box box. We are only learning, after all. It is noon. We have consumed our federally subsidized noon-meal milk in the cafeteria downstairs, slid our trays down the rollerpath to an unseen steamy clatter, come upstairs to the gym as have generations, with or without the federal milk, before us in this town, and the new and handsome and young boys' gym teacher jockeys the discs, new 45's, and the same dark-eyed boy always gathers his strength and always asks me and always relieved, I always accept, so we are, both of us, more or less dancing.

Familiar faces warmed by swipes of greasestick, the Indian troop performs. The drum begins, slowly almost inperceptibly growing out of our hearts; the brand touches the twin teepees of kindling atop the ceremonial fire and with a rush the small flames hurry to burn downward; the dancers space themselves, their feathers, their rawhide, their fringes and beads, out; toe-heel, toe-heel, each step a minute portion faster than the one before it, they follow the music as it grows with each striking on the drum a minute portion louder than the sound before it; as the fire blazes the dancers begin to whirl, first one arm up and then the other, rattles in the air buzzing; the quills quiver and the beads whisper and the fringed leather whistles in the air until the loud has become loudest and the quickness is quickest and the reds and oranges grow until the fire crashes in on itself and blazes higher than ever until with a shout and a last hard thud the drum is done, the chanting chanted and in the yellow light we can see that the dance has been danced.

To have danced. Oh, to have danced is to have lived. Some do, some do not. We have not: we are the race's freaks, the spindlies, gawks, awkwards, the clumsies of the species, handicapped by our tremendous size. Miserable, we seek company in misery equal to our own. It is the law of the jungle. We gather, we order our drinks, which we hope will help us be beautiful. We watch the many-mirrored globe turn. The lighting is out of a bad movie. Even with those perpetually out-of-place, I am out of place. Around me are shiny serge and clingy rayon, mechanics and checkers in supermarkets and vacations in Wisconsin Dells, someday. They want above all to dance the all-important dance, and dancing is beginning to look silly to me. I dance instead with their desire to dance, their compulsion, their im-

which is at once the secret of life and art. Fresh joy in the idea of repetition. To the music of the electronic flute, the heart of art spins the copies out, again again again, and unless the power fails there's no stopping her dancing.

Our teacher has been packed with remarkable skill into a surprised angora sweater and a straight skirt approaching the parallel, which has been fitted with an inverted pleat at the rear just below the knees to facilitate dancing. We are in the fifties and in the seventh grade. The war is over, the USO has been condemned and soon will be torn down, but for the moment we are committed to ten (10) lessons in ballroom dancing there, after school on Tuesdays. Our teacher is a blonde. She wears extreme calculations of eye makeup. Our teacher has, we have been informed ahead of time, a lot of personality. We are trying desperately to have a lot of personality as well, for we sense a lot of personality is crucial to being a social success. We are resolved to watch this person closely, to see what exactly is meant by a lot of personality. We are diligence. We are in fact Girl Scouts and as such have given our solemn word that we will try. The first thing we learn is that half of us must be boys: we must learn to lead, though a girl must never ever lead her partner unless she can do so with such subtlety he will never guess. Learning to lead will be good practice, we are told, so we will know what not to do. It is impolite to refuse a cut-in, we learn, however impolite the cut-in might seem, or to discuss politics or religion on the dance floor. Minds on our feet, we cultivate the aphoristic style. Today we learn the two-step. Two steps forward, one step back, progressing sideways. Use your imaginations, girls, the teacher tells us; don't just go in a straight line. Variety, she says, is the secret of the good dancer. Dancing becomes the goal, the grail. If only we could keep from going in a straight line, if only we had a lot of personality. Next week, our teacher tells us, we'll learn the box, but between now and then we should practice. Get our brother (I have none) or our father (whose heavenly dancing has such variety I never was to learn to keep up with him) and practice! That's the key to success. The weeks stretch out golden and promising and angora before us: the fox trot, the rhumba, the samba, the polka, the viennese waltz, oh joy the tango roses in our teeth, and finally, if we're very good, the lindy, the jitterbug and all the variations thereon. We try, oh how we try, and we watch for emanations of personality, which seem to be inextricably bound up with eye makeup and tightness and the ability to talk well about nothing and variousness as one proceeds to dance.

Out of the night they came, the pledge-class walkouts from Urbana. En masse in the cavernous foyer of Main Hall, they melt their snowy shoes into the ridges of black rubber runner that crosses the entryway, joining the verandah's big double doors with the mirrored swinging doors that lead upstairs to the freshman dormitory. TWENTY. The word came over the second floor main phone. Some of us were already spoken for, had established fresh liasons with boys from the college across town or enticed old steadies to visit weekends. Twenty, they said, the request relayed by the switchboard operator who wore her hair pulled tight and had one shoe with a thick sole. Twenty customers for the mixer in the rathskeller. Twenty minutes. The cashmere sweaters fly out of twenty drawers, the low heels walk out of twenty closets, the pearls circle twenty necks, Chanel clouds twenty rooms. Purses, gloves, mouton jackets, cigarettes, badges. Twenty dancing women, tight as an infantry squadron, descend the stairs, pass through the mirrored doors, and on the black river to the night meet their partners for the dance.

I never saw him before, and I never saw him again after. I don't remember his name, and I am not sure he even told me. The idea was not to care about things like names, not to look as though anything mattered very much. We lit pack after pack of cigarettes, being exceptionally cool; we stared into gallons of Coke, being cool, studied walls and ceilings with an infinite absorption. The fact remains: decades later I remember his dancing. Whirler par excellence. Even though everyone was supposed to be cool, people watched. When we had finished, though, we had finished. He didn't come back, and of course he couldn't and mustn't. The melancholy was a large part of it all. The dance, over, was sufficient in its having been danced.

The grandfather of all grandfathers points his finger down on top of my head like a lathe. I spin, knocking bits of air away. Turn, turn, he says, and his slippered foot keeps time with the music only he can hear, long-ago far-away vaudeville music. The grandfather of all grandfathers was an Indian, a Senator, a Tiger. On the road he met the singers and dancers of his time, some as famous as he was. They had dinners together. Nights he would watch them sing and dance; days, they would watch him play ball. He was the premier danseur, the pitcher, the holder of the ball, decider of what happened when, who would pump and kick and hurl arms and legs and sliders and spit-balls and curves and changeups and fastballs and sinkers and dusters, Long Bob had a cool head, they said, week after week, summer after summer, year after year. And now in his head he pitches, while on his finger I dance.

Squat was the only way to describe him. Short legs was what you noticed first, seeing him full-length, proportions all wrong, and broad in the beam as well. The stories spun out of his mouth like webs catching all who listened, occasionally catching him as well. New York New York New York, seventeen and in New York, a student of the dance, a scholar of the maestro tap tap tapping on the stairway to the stars, flap ball change shuffle shuffle turn and wing wing wing and here we are years later nowhere. In his bachelor apartment far from New York, observing the folly of trying too hard. In his three-piece khaki corduroy, high-collared buttondown oxford, rep tie, he dances the dance of years ago with professional ease, though with certain theatrical embellishments that are out of place here and everywhere. Dancing is his life, poor fellow, and embarrassed, we say what we know we have to: Gee, you're a terrific dancer.

Wordless among the bedclothes, we are the frieze on the temple, the decorations around the vase, the chiaroscuro of a round dance that will become the Hours of Charles d'Angouleme. Wordless, my children left-foot, right-foot, forward, backward, inward, outward, turn-about. Wordless, we are everyone spontaneous, we are joy, we are ritual, we are human contrivance against the fates and elements; we spin into delirium, into wishful thought, into passionate stupors. Wordless, we press against our partners, dancing into the night, out of the dawn, over cliffs. Wordless, we clasp hands in a circle and dance.

The Deposition

They tell me I will have to forget about it or I will end up as crazy as the man I killed. It is good advice. I can see the wisdom in it. But their wisdom has forgotten to tell me the one important thing: how. However wise, theirs is an uninformed opinion. They do not have all the facts, especially the most important. That in a secret way I have always known or planned it, but if I tell anyone that they'll swear I have truncated the process and hit the true and absolute dead end sooner than anyone dreamed possible. Dreaming is what it's all about, bad dreaming, bad dreams. No, the dream murder was not the way it finally happened in real life, but the idea was always there, a bad ambition from the underside of sleep, my slightly disguised certainty that I would inexorably kill or maim and it would be inexplicable and I would end my days in a fumble for words. And so I have and am. Someone else has found my voice and is using it for me, giving the official version. It is just as well, for I do not remember exactly what happened.

The night was dark, she says. It is a beginning. Everyone has been very nice to me, perhaps too nice, certainly nicer than they should be, nicer than they would be if they knew me the way I do. I, playing the avenging angel at the wheel of my homocidal car, miraculous instrument of faith, the fate-bundle. I am no innocent. It is not the first time: once one August a dog. No witnesses. This there is no hiding, however, no minimizing, though for my sake now they are trying to minimize. Positing values they call it in some circles. Everyone present says they know it could not be called my fault, that the man I have killed has been a nuisance in this town for years, a public joke and a disgrace to his family, a hazard on the streets for pedestrians and drivers alike, a source of confusion for one and all. I cry and will *not cry.* They tell me I must go on.

She dabs her eyes and says, *I was traveling east on Route 13.* If I had made it up the number would be more comfortable; if I had made my whole life up, it wouldn't have seemed less real. Our lies are real, the real becomes the ultimate falsehood, and the truth fits in nowhere. The lies everyone talks about here are the lies people told to make the town forget who he really was, this man I killed, to keep them from remembering his name. The police give me the absolute and unalterable facts. That he had never been seen or remembered to converse with another human. That he kept his sacred hybrid bicycle in a constant state of flux, modifying it with the seasons and whatever spare part came his way on the dump. That he lived in a tarpaper shack of his own strange design at the dump like some hobo. That he was a problem to the community. Bad example. Unwholesome influence.

She answers, *About forty or forty-five miles an hour. Maybe I should have been going slower.* The chief of police presses his mouth together hard and shakes his head NO. You must relax, he tells me, we all knew it would happen one day sooner or later. It was just a matter of time. Think of yourself as an instrument of God's will, sweetheart, which he didn't say but meant. God's will: a dark night, a car traveling, proper lane, proper speed, proper highway, and down from the cemetery driveway, Walnut Hill Second Addition it turned out, with a whoop, indians attacking the wagon train, he came, no hands, winter chat churning and the squirreltail on the handlebar cracking in the January cold, and I heard him whoop, a bird nearing extinction. Extinction, and I would not explain it to myself. I knew it but I would not believe it, the dream memory confirmed. *That* was how it really happened, but it all seems so preposterous. Even if they are willing to believe it, I am not. They shake their heads, sooner or later, sooner or later, someone from out of town who didn't know him and his haunts and his ways of darting out into traffic like that would end it once and for all, sooner or later. Later I saw the oogha horn, crushed. I hadn't heard it. He died of a broken neck, like a bird that flew into glass.

I saw a blur, she confides to the chief, *dark-colored and metal, coming from the right. I heard a whoop.* Relax, the police chief says to me. The chief tells me, sympathetically, who he is, and he is the dead man's second cousin. That I have nothing to fear from him, that he wants me to know that, that there will be no prosecution, no official inquiry, that he is here to do what he can to help me. That the man had no family other than some second cousins, of which he is one, and some greatnieces and nephews of which his dead cousin's far away children are some, and that there is nothing for me to worry about, that no one could possibly hold me responsible for what happened, for his erratic behavior. All is forgiven, go home. Thank you, big chief. If I would like he will arrange for his family physician to see me, to perhaps admit me to the local hospital so I can get some rest after such a shock. The righthand captain nods. It might not be a bad idea, he says. Stone walls do not a prison make nor iron bars, a hospital. How much do they know, these people?

A thud and I put on the brakes and knew it was too late, that what I hit must have been a person but I couldn't believe it, the deponent sayeth. A tired old saw, that knowing-believing thing. Where do they think I have been all of my life? Every town has a person like that. If I had known I was passing a graveyard. He took to hanging out around there, says Mr. Righthand, last summer. Oh, we run him off every chanct we got, but you can't put a car out at Walnut Hill twenty-four hours a day, not when you got the kind of problems we got in this town. What kind is that, I wonder. Every time I found him there, says the captain, he was reciting something memorized. Foreign poems or something. Never said a word to me or anybody I ever heard tell, but we heard him talk plenty. He'd like to never shut up. Enter the death-dealing angel, specializing in silencing the eternally loquacious. Old guy would sit up there on the biggest stone in the graveyard and once said a poem I even recognized. Thanotopsis, by William Cullen Bryant, had to memorize part of it myself in seventh grade and never will forget it, only he remembered what must have been the whole thing.

I couldn't look, couldn't move. Except to turn on the blinkers. Emergency. Funny, they make a tiny pinging sound, those distress lights. I never used them before; there just had never been any emergencies. And now the pinging and January with no snow and lights dotting the dark. No wind. Bent dead grass along the right of way just before the cemetery begins. Trees black maps in the sky. Hardly enough moon to see by. Enough moon to have seen him, missed him? The chief bothers me without meaning to. His being here disturbs me, his comforting me when it is his own flesh and blood I caused the end of. Things are backwards. It is as though I have done them a favor. *The oak shall send his roots abroad, and pierce thy mould,* I remember.

She is forgetting the details but tells them, *I remained in the car—it was so quiet.* They have talked it over. For my own good, general agreement all around, the wisdom of the collection. The chief goes to call the doctor. The game is a new one on the market, called Compassion. Or is it Guile. Perhaps they suspect what I am thinking, the dreams I am remembering. But yes, I will go to the hospital, just for overnight, just to rest. Yes, I will. To sleep. I will forget and not dream the dream.

I heard nothing, it was done. Not even dead poetry in the night. No cries of pain. I knew the man on the bicycle must be dead. He didn't communicate with anybody, the chief said. It had been years. I would send him his tax form and never get any response, the chief said, so I had to take to signing for him, had him declared NCM, power of attorney and all. Spinning his web across the road, just like that, caught and I am caught too, the cobweb is sticky, will release no one. He'd wander into the bookstore over at the college, the chief said remembering as he spoke, find a new book, pay for it, leave, never say a word to anybody. A real odd duck. The doctor, Harrison, arrives, looks into my eyes, makes a phone call and says, You just need some rest. Everything will be all right in the morning.

'I think I've killed a man, officer, a man on a bicycle.' New equation: it is an old town, that much I can see in the night. Row houses. Brick. German, 1840's, 1860's. Yards tidy, hedges clipped. A positive disgrace, he was, the matron is saying to me. She is fat, hanging out over, bursting through her uniform, exceeding the belt, the collar, the skirt, the shoes. Too much stollen, liebchen. They think she will comfort me. I'd sooner be by myself. Funny thing, the comfort lady says, always kept to himself, but he was always right in the middle of things. Once, she remembered, when Kennedy spoke on the courthouse steps.... I turn the cushionlady's voice off. I don't want to hear about the man hearing Johnson or Goldwater or Kennedy or any-

body. Their causes are dead entities, forgotten, and her memories might as well be bogus.

Yes, I would like to get some sleep, but I don't think I can. I have forgotten how. Head on the pillow. Eyes closed. See the sheep? Perhaps what they are giving me is truth serum and I will tell them all about knowing it was going to happen one day and they will begin to think I really could have stopped after all. What does it matter. I will tell them all. Medication. Premeditation. I knew it would happen, just as I knew this would happen. Voices far away, She's fighting it. Fighting the wheel. Relax, go limp. Legs floating, hands in the sky, the air is water, the feathers grow, new sky, higher. Another 5 cc's ought to do it. Achtung! Wir haben hier....

My lover. He doesn't shave regularly, and a dusting of silver whiskers sparkles along his jaw. Let me give you a haircut, I tell him. He looks up and speaks. No. I like my hair like this. Well, I should have known. One does not intrude into another's life and immediately propose a haircut. Delilah, Samson, Absalom, Achitophel. We talk. Would you like to see my headdress, he offers. I smile yes and he hauls up from the clutter on the floor a leather aviator's helmet, ears gone blank, the chin strap worn away to nothing. Wait, he says, that's not the whole thing. He brings out a pair of horse's blinders and fits them on his head. There, how do you like it? He takes off the headgear and laughs. He speaks in many languages, every comment being in a new language; so far we have had french, italian, russian, portuguese. I answer him in german and he is silent. He tugs his frayed sweater close to him and rearranges the pen that peeks out of its collar. A diller, a dollar, a five o'clock scholar. A stone. Only poetry, he finally says. The germ'z are condemned henceforth to poetry. Let the punishment fit the crime, I say, not thinking. He recites Goethe. Fliegentod. We look into each other's eyes and I ask him, Why do you live like this. If it's money, I begin. He laughs. He laughs. He laughs. I would have you know, he says, I *do* it for the money, and he begins to dance around the tarpaper shack. The night is cold for August, but August nights in these parts have been known to be very cold. A dusting of silver sparkles outside on the dump. His silverchrome elaborated bicycle is at the ready, and I am afraid he will leave me. Still he laughs and he goes over and pulls out the grey volume of Sappho and holds it by the spine sideways. A snow of money, fifty-dollar bills, ones, hundreds, tens, twenties, checks. L'argent, c'est rien. And he laughs again and this time smiles and when he laughs I can see his teeth and they are silver and they are diamonds and they are glistening in the frosty evening, the frozen dew of August. Another book and another. You see, he demands with a mock gruffness. He scuffs through the money on the floor, kicking up dustdevils of salaries and I wonder why, if it means so little to him, he would not give it to someone it could help. I would not dare to ask him now, perhaps later. Out of the applecrate comes a matched pair of jellyglasses. He muses to himself, rummaging among the debris in the corner. When he turns around, he has a bottle of wine, an unacknowledged but great vintage. To warm us against the chill of the night, he says with a buffoon's bow and in a language I am surprised to find myself understanding. Let us drink and tell each other the stories of our lives, he says, whether they are real or not. The stories, the lives? I love his ambiguities and possibly I love him. No longer am I me, dried up on the inside, wrinkling on the outside, going on forty-five. I am seventeen or twenty-two and he is timeless, the way some men ever are and women never can be. My hands are smooth and strong, the knots untied, my mind free as an April storm and we are swept along, the wonderful wine. It is any season we wish, any year we wish: all things are possible here on the dump with the bicycle man. The dump is all things, the bicycle man all men. For a moment I forget myself. As he pours the second glass of wine for me I remember that I do not know his name, that he does not know my name. It is, of course, better that way. Why should we bother with names in a society of two? We are babies, primal self and other, and bothering with more is a waste of time. His hair grows in wild curls. Silver. He begins his story: I remember nothing, it is important that you remember that. Did I just tell you I remember nothing? He laughs. You must remember nothing, too, he tells me. Of this you will remember nothing or almost nothing, though you will try hard to keep hold of the picture, the words, the night, the taste of the wine, the color of frost. Forgetting is the essence of living, remembering is the curse. Remember that, he says and kisses me and laughs. Crickets, I think. I will remember the crickets on the dump. I tell him. Suit yourself, he says. It's your funeral. He laughs and recites another snatch of Goethe: *Sie fühlt sich wohl, und....* Where did you learn, I begin and stop myself without the question mark. Shell shock, perhaps. I don't remember, he says, I told you. You must remember to forget. But your accent, I say. Ah, at the knee of my grandmother, he says. I remember the knee of my grandmother, and a fat knee it was, and the knee of my grandfather, a fine horse. So you see, I forgot that I remembered. Perhaps there are other things you remember, I venture. Not bloody likely, he says, and turns to look out across the dump. Why should I remember anything, with this—his hand passes in front of the bookcases, sweeps the dump. I go forth daily, he tells me. I wander into the world and forget it immediately. Cain. Absalom. Ishmael. Everyday on my bicycle up and down the streets of whatever wilderness this is, I've forgotten. Filling my saddlebags with the priceless debris of the world, the discarded and forgotten. People think, people say, it's just the village crazy, out for a joy ride. How should they know what I am looking for? How should I know—I forget. But I look. I look. I look for what I forget and forget what I find. I am lost in the clauses. He laughs and empties the bottle. Outside on the dump other voices. Very far away but getting closer. I wish they'd leave me alone, he says. I wish they'd all get lost, forget me, forget themselves, forget to breathe, maybe. He laughs and the voices grow louder, the words more distinct. Their talk takes on form: *here* and *asleep* and *tonight*. Anxious I drink the last of my wine. I feel very very tired; the cover on his bed is scratchy cheap wool that picks up dark glimmers in its fibers and my eyes close, though I have not started the story of my life and I seem to remember we didn't get very far on his. Don't forget, he says, as I am falling asleep, forget. He laughs. Forget.

...her to understand that we want to forget all about it. Incessant whispering, all dumb talk. Someone has gotten in the shack, an interloper. Talking in the corner there by his books and this is a hospital and I have slept. No. I will forget how to wake up; I am going back to the dump where I belong. I will show them. We will open another bottle of wine and go on with the story. We will recite Rilke and Goethe and Schiller and read each other all of Mann and Proust and whatever suits your silver fancy, it's your dump and that counts for everything. Der Konig in Thule. Forget, forget. She can go anytime she wants, says someone in the dark, a nurse most probably.

Domestic Help

She talked to herself. A lot and loudly. Held two-sided conversations with her husbands, neither present and one of them dead. Didn't fold the towels the way Helen showed her—the big bath towels like this, she had said, folding the towel in half, then in quarters the same way, and then in thirds, widthwise. Insisted on folding them half and half and half, and nothing fit in the linen drawers. Had made a fetish of putting Helen's French ceramic ovenware on top of the stove, heating it with too little water or dry food in it, letting the bottoms scorch for all time. Could not be trained to iron shirts as Charles wanted them. Could not even be taught to walk without scuffing her feet. She was everywhere when Helen wished she'd just fade into the woodwork, and nowhere to be found when there was something to locate or an errand to run. Belle was, in a word, impossible.

"Where did you dig this one up, Mother?" Helen's daughter Gloria had asked. The girl's question had sounded like a rebuke: *You've done it again, Mother.*

And how could Helen explain? "Domestic help is impossible these days," she finally said. "No one wants to do that kind of work."

"Mother. Where did you get her?"

"The state employment agency," Helen replied, finally. Any explanation would be as much for her own benefit as Gloria's. Helen's friends hadn't been interested in having her lure their help away; no one had known of a soul. "At least the people the state sends need to work," she added lamely. Needing to work and wanting to were two different things, though Belle had, at first, seemed willing enough.

"I say she's bad news, Mother, and I say ditch her. The sooner the better." Gloria and her opinions, Helen thought, trying to remember that the help was hers, not Gloria's, however nearly keeping Gloria's room straight might approach being a full-time occupation. God help the man who marries her, Helen thought, or give him money enough to have help. Gloria was back to filing her nails, making Helen wonder how fast nails could possibly grow, with all that filing.

"She's going to steal you blind, Mother," Gloria insisted. "Now I can't find my best silk scarf. Poof! If Belle weren't such an elephant, I'd be missing a whole lot more."

Cornered. Helen didn't like having to defend Belle, didn't like making the excuse that the scarf would turn up. She suspected it might not, and it didn't.

Come May, Belle would be with Helen for ten years. And the longer Belle was with her, the more she had to admit it: maybe Gloria had been right on the mark after all. There had been the predictable, trivial annoyances, the kinds of things that always come with less-than-careful help. Banged furniture, colors run in the laundry, the need to constantly prod. Aside from that, Helen always had the feeling that Belle was scurrying off, afternoons, under a cloud of probable misfeasance. People had to accept a certain amount of pilferage —food, mainly. But the other things troubled Helen, the littler, more subtle things, the little oddments, the totems that stood between lady and servant. Never anything very valuable. The dregs of an expensive bottle of perfume. The small, seemingly insignificant souvenirs of trips Helen and Charles had taken. Gloria still complained, more so now that she was married and running her own house, on the subject of That Awful Belle, who now did Gloria's heavy work, more or less, one day a week—how odd it was that "freaky things," as Gloria put it, would grow legs and walk off. Gloria's housekeeping would never change, Helen thought. Such a messy girl.

Belle's talking grew more and more blatant. At first it had been confined to barely audible mumbling in empty rooms, just now and then. Helen had at first come upon Belle exhorting the fuzz bunnies under Gloria's bed or entreating closetfuls of clothes. And earnestly, as though *they* could, for all the world, understand and respond to every word she said. While she ironed Charles' shirts, she excoriated her husband Pete, and mankind in general. When she ran the vacuum, her children caught hell in no uncertain terms. "Tina, how many times have I told you! When will you get the sense God gave you!" Belle's religious allusions grew in pace with the multiplication of her troubles.

Four or five years ago now, Belle had come to Helen in the midst of the household bills. "Need to talk to you," she telegraphed characteristically. Helen continued writing the sewer-tax check and made a point of not looking up.

"What is it, Belle?" What is it this time, she wondered. How much does she want? What is the fresh catastrophe?

Without an invitation, Belle seated herself across the desk from Helen. "Pete," she said. Her husband. Now what? Belle's first hints at trouble between them had been so gentle as to be practically unnoticeable, the sort of thing one could turn aside with barely a comment. I have enough trouble of my own, Helen always thought on hearing of others' domestic woes, without borrowing somebody else's troubles. But the hints had become lunch-time anecdotes which grew steadily to full-blown horror stories, impossible to turn aside with "Too bad." Helen had always wondered why Belle needed to work; Pete was a crane-operator who made good money and ought to be more than able to care for his family comfortably. "No," Belle had said, "don't want me to work, don't like it one bit. More I try and do, more trouble, worsen he is. Just don't like me having no money of my own." Pete was taking to extravagances beyond his means—very expensive cars, TVs with four-foot screens, Belle didn't know what all. "Can't figure out what that guy does with money, lessen he eats it."

Belle across the desk disquieted Helen. "I've got a ton of work here, Belle, and I can't put it off." Belle stuck tight in the chair.

"Don't know what to do with Pete, Miss Helen. Swear to God I don't." Belle began to cry, snuffling loudly. Crocodile tears, Helen thought, but immediately felt guilty for suspecting Belle. She was obviously in a bad way.

"If it will just take a minute..."

Belle pounced. "Just can't take no more, Miss Helen. Can't. There's limits. If I don't get outen that house, take my kids and get, something terrible's.... Pete, he's been beating on them. Ain't done nothing wrong. Takes it in his crazy head to whop them, asks them something, nice and sweet, and when they open their mouth to answer, he up and hits them. They don't give him no sass, none."

Helen felt cornered, always cornered with this Belle. "I don't know what to tell you, Belle. I try never to put my nose in anyone's marriage. Every chicken has her own nest to tend." Belle snuffled again, louder.

Belle stood. "Want to show you something. Look at this, Miss Helen." Belle turned, pulling up the back of her blouse. There across her back were what at first looked like the clawmarks of a giant cat. Red, spaced stripes on pale flesh that made Helen draw her breath sharply. Things like this didn't really happen. Things like this happen in the soaps, in cheap fiction, not to real people. The evidence of Pete's cruelty confounded her; Helen couldn't find words. Belle lowered her blouse and turned.

"That's not all," she said. As Belle unbuttoned the cuffs of her sleeves, Helen remembered thinking that morning how odd that Belle had on long sleeves in all this heat. Belle pulled up one sleeve and then the other to reveal haphazard bandages on both forearms. On the right, some of the gauze was a faint dull red, through its several layers.

"That's what Pete done," Belle said, peculiarly triumphant.

"But how? Why would anyone do such a thing?" Helen found herself stammering questions she didn't really want the answers to.

"Don't ask me. Just mean. Crazy. First he done my back, withen a belt. Then he come after me with the knife." The rush of tears seemed genuine, warranted.

"A knife?"

"Butcher. Laying on the countertop. Just started off swinging with it. Kids was outside, thank the Lord."

"Did you go to a doctor, Belle? To the emergency room? How bad are those cuts?"

"Not that deep. No, no doctor. Questions. All innocent, 'How'd this happen?' they'd say. Iffen I really told them, they'd call in the cops. He'd really kill me then."

If this sort of thing keeps up, he very well may, Helen reflected, but she couldn't say it, with Belle hysterical as it was. Helen gave her a moment to calm herself, to not much avail. "Has Pete ever done anything like this before?" she finally asked.

"Not like this. Hands and fists before, all right, lots. But not with no strap. Or no knife. But this is the end. I got to do something."

"But what?"

"That's what I mean to ask you, Miss Helen. I never believed in divorces—seems like they go against God—till now. I got no choice. I know you got a cousin's a lawyer."

Belle was right, but Ned was in tax, not domestic practice. Helen waited, and so did Belle. "He doesn't do that kind of law work, Belle. I don't think he'd make any exception." Belle didn't hide her disappointment.

"Well, then, maybe he knows of somebody, a good lawyer to look after my interests, and the kids'." Belle certainly could come right to the point when she wanted to. She winced as she touched the tape that held down the bandage on her right arm, trying to get it re-stuck. Then she turned her blonde, frizzy head down so that Helen couldn't see her face. The whole thing embarrassed Helen, and she was relieved not to have any more of Belle to sort out for the moment.

And so Belle had made the move from talking to herself to talking to Helen. Belle's was a relatively routine divorce, thanks to the evidence Pete had provided, and since the lawyer Ned recommended got Belle a generous settlement, Helen thought she had heard the end of Belle's troubles. But the end of one kind of trouble spelled the beginning of another, unguessed at.

Helen didn't know what she would do with Charles. He's acting like such a baby, one side of her said, but she had to admit she didn't know how adult her reaction would be if the doctors told her she had cancer. The prognosis was excellent, they all said. Or did they always say that? You're one of the lucky ones, they told Charles; we caught it early; you're going to come through this just fine. That was eight years ago, and the doctors hadn't been entirely right. Something the doctors called "iffy" showed up in a routine checkup; they wanted to do a big operation. Charles refused. He would take cobalt treatments, but nothing more. Charles retired.

Not just from his business, which he handed over to Helen to run completely—though she had been doing so, in essence, for several years—but from life in general. He hid in the house. Characters on the soaps became his friends, their myriad dilemmas and infidelities and their far-fetched involvements in deceit and murder became the staples of his thinking, Charles' obsessive concerns. Real life receded from Charles, and Helen worried about the change in him. "Let's go out for a lobster, Charles," she would suggest, remembering how many times they'd done so together, happily. "Not up to it," Charles would inevitably say, and finally it seemed Charles was not up to going out of the house for any reason whatsoever.

Helen resented his childish demands, and still she felt sorry for him. What had happened to the Charles she married? Had years and events changed her as much as they'd changed him? Where was Charles the hell-raiser, the fellow with all that zest and enthusiasm? The panache was gone. He stared at the TV. Helen couldn't tell whether his lack of response was due to mental deterioration, an absorption with the soap opera of the moment, or a fear of taking her suggestion, doing what he should do, going in for a checkup. He'd made last-minute excuses for the last four, and didn't even call the doctor to say he wasn't coming. What used to be all fight was now flight. Charles always had such a good tan, somehow all year round, but now he was pale and putting on weight from not doing anything but lying on the couch, watching TV, snoozing off and on all day.

"I don't think you really heard me, Charles," she said, thinking she must sound like a shrew these days. She ought to watch her tone.

"Heard you," a voice said, disembodied. It didn't sound like Charles, or even as if it came from him.

"Don't you think it's just about time for a checkup? Don't you think it would be a good idea, to be on the safe side?"

Charles' eyes remained on the TV screen. The remote control rested on his stomach. "Not really."

"How do you feel?"

"OK."

"Well, good. Maybe we could...."

"I'm not going anywhere. I'm just fine where I am."

"But you've got to get up and move some. Lying around like this all day is terrible for you. It's no wonder you can't sleep at night, Charles. Dr. McIntyre says he's not giving you any more sleeping pills until you come in and see him."

"He just wants a guinea pig. I'll get my own sleeping pills. I don't need him or any of those other quacks."

"You're being silly. You need a prescription for those pills." Where did Charles think he could get sleeping pills—the black market? Did pushers offer home-delivery these days? Charles barely made sense these days. He never initiated conversations anymore, and most of the talking he did was with Belle. Only it wasn't really talking. Silly chit-chat. Helen would overhear them sometimes, the same dull jokes over and over, which hardly qualified as real conversation. Helen wasn't imagining things: Charles was a totally different person. Anything that smacked of repetition had always bored him. Now he took some strange kind of comfort in familiar patter, predictable retorts, time and time again the same.

"Maybe another doctor?" she finally ventured. "Or another kind of doctor, perhaps?"

For the first time in days he looked away from the TV and straight at Helen.

"What's that supposed to mean?"

"Nothing in particular, I was just thinking...."

"I know what you're thinking, Helen. You think you're going to get me to go to some shrink. You don't fool me for one minute."

"I'm not trying to fool you," she told Charles, but she knew he should talk to someone, since he obviously wasn't talking to her. "What could it hurt?"

"I've got news for you, Helen. I'm not looney, and I'm not going to talk to some shrink. I know what happens to those people, get old and sick like me. Put them away in some hospital and call them nuts, and pretty soon they are. That kills people, you know."

"Who says they would put you in a hospital? Look, I'll go with you. We could all talk together, if it would make you feel better. Maybe it doesn't have to be a doctor—maybe that young fellow at the church, Reverend Weller."

"My problems are none of his business. I'm not going. That's final."

What could anyone do for someone who refused to accept help, who refused to do the least thing to help himself? Charles infuriated her. "Just how do you think you're going to get sleeping pills?" she shot at him, the sound of her voice shrill, harsher than she thought it could be.

"Never mind," he said. "I'll get the pills."

And he did. Though at first Helen couldn't figure out how, she finally put two and two together, and came up with Belle. The assortment of ailments that plagued Belle, her children, and people of her immediate acquaintance defied the imagination, or at least Helen's. Helen had learned to be reluctant to greet Belle in the morning with an inquiry after her health—too many times she had done so and been waylaid for up to an hour with a blow-by-blow description of someone's trip to some specialist, for some statistically improbable ailment. Now Helen had an office to run, but Belle did her level best to see that Helen had a good dose of jeremiad before she got off, and of course before the bathroom floor got washed. I am being conned, Helen often felt, marvelling at how, when Belle came to her for the day's special instructions, the conversation could always be turned to the latest atrocity or medical emergency. Just like the soaps. Helen chided herself for her lack of sympathy with Belle's ongoing woes, and for her inability to keep the situation under control. Who was mistress of this house, after all? Who was Belle to heap all that clinical saga on her?

"Mother, when are you going to learn?" Gloria asked her. "Belle is totally out of hand. Tell her to shape up or ship out."

But now Belle's doctors and their nurses filled the air around where she dusted and swept and scrubbed. She spoke with receptionists and demanded an earlier appointment. She ordered double quantities of prescriptions, despite the doctor's orders. She checked and double-checked on the results of laboratory tests, placing indignant solo calls to see if x-rays had been read, if the hematology department was minding its p's and q's. Into the rooms of Helen's house she poured all the complaints known and unknown to man, so that Helen could feel the air becoming thick with sickness and pain and fear, making her uncomfortable when she was home and distressed when she was away for fear of what new calamity of the imagination might just have become part of the fabric of Charles' surroundings. Some terrible unheard-of disease, a cluster of contradictory symptoms. Drug reactions, close calls. Insomnia. Fatigue. The lamentations and malaises filled, it seemed to Helen, every last crevice and closet, every nook and cranny.

She caught them, more or less, in the act, though Helen wasn't positive what act it was precisely, and though both of them would later deny that they were doing anything improper. That would go without saying. Whatever they were doing it didn't look to Helen as though it was right; on the contrary, it gave the appearance of being very wrong. Whatever was happening would have to be measured in terms of the appearance, in terms of her coming upon a man and a woman whose faces were familiar but whom she didn't really know, of the daybed cushions awry, of them straightening their clothes hurriedly, of a rising flush coming to the faces of two chronically and mortally ill persons. She would somehow deal with the appearance, come to terms with it, but for the moment she went to her bedroom and locked them out, away from her, so their disease could not touch her, and she sat down on the smooth, uncrumpled sheets and blankets and spread of the king-sized bed, where she asked herself how she had come to be the help in her own house.

Creatures of This Place

I have come to visit Texas, the Bayou country. If I sit here the whole week and look at it, it won't impress me any more than it does right now, and right now I am not impressed. It was foolish to come.

It will be beautiful, he said. It will be grand.

We will have the house all to ourselves, he said.

He didn't mention the roaches, even though hereabouts even the best houses have roaches, he tells me. He didn't mention the spiders. Or the mosquitoes that scream in my ears all night long. And he didn't mention the peculiar cat, which he calls Tortoise, that pokes its face at me from its place on top the air conditioner, staring in the window there, when I'm dressing or whatever, with its face divided just like that.

A cat whose face is divided like that makes me try to remember an old maxim, one that warns a person off.

The cat has just done a beastly thing. It has killed the little lizard that has been playing the last few days in the ivy around the window. The cat has taunted the lizard with claw pricks, and I never really saw how it was the cat killed the lizard. Whether it cracked its spine with a bite or not, I do not know. I am not sure the cat could kill with just the claw pricks. But it has killed. The lizard is quite dead.

And now the cat looks in at me through the grimy sash that hasn't been lowered to be washed for—how many years. It is saying something to me, but I cannot hear its words.

Its whiskers lean forward, then twitch.

I feel the spiders and roaches are watching me too. They are creatures of this place, and this place is his.

I should never have come, but I have said I would stay the week and if I am to keep my sanity in the meantime, I must give order to what happens and occupy myself with other than straight thinking. I hope he does not find me doing this. I have never seen Jordan mad, but I suspect that he has a terrible temper when it gets set off. People who laugh easily are usually terribly violent, and he laughs easily. He has never been mad at me, but he probably would be if he saw this.

The real irony of my situation is I'm not sure, basically, how or why I got into it. I agreed to come. To visit his home. To meet his friends. To see places he always talks of. To meet his family. I remember details well, but details are not basics.

I do not want to go to the beach and look at grains of sand. Infinities depress me.

I do not want to go to the beach and look at the innards of the ocean, the men of war.

I would perhaps enjoy a walk through the dunes, where the surf's roar is not so loud.

They tell me there is a kind of grass called sea oats that has a poetic function. The sea oats establish quickly and they stabilize the dune. The sea oats grow on the top of the dune. Once it is certain the dune will not blow away, the other plants crowd the sea oats out. Perhaps I do not want to see the sea oats.

Once before I saw the innards of the ocean on the beach and did not know what they were. They looked like great multi-baby-colored unstuffed sausages. Some kind of living tissue balloon with all this improbable blue glop hanging off one side. They littered the beach. The ocean had a party, and this was the garbage. Then I saw a long line of pickup trucks way down the beach, coming toward me. They swerved right and left. The soft sand, I thought. Then I could see they were deliberately cutting back and forth across the beach. The lead pickup truck was heading for the biggest jellyfish it could find. Those that it missed, one following would hit.

When the trucks ran over the jellyfish, they popped the air sacs. It was a game. The men of war sounded like gentle firecrackers.

The footprints of the birds were numerous.

It would be better to go to the beach again than to go back to anywhere where his friends are. I am supposed to be thoroughly impressed, with this house with its roaches and spiders and murderous cat, with the land, with the pictures of his father being decorated as commodore of the local coast guard auxiliary, with his mother's scrapbooks from trips around the world. I look out at what remains of the land sold off little by little, and I am not impressed. He has driven with me out to the limits of what used to be their land, what his mother inherited, and I would not be proud. I would keep it a secret. What I would keep a secret and what I would be proud of matters little to him, and that is why there is little reason to be here.

I really cannot understand it, why he has me here. What has he planned for me—why has he brought me to this place?

Perhaps he plans to kill me and feed me to the minnows in the bayou. Perhaps I will fertilize, unannounced, the roots of some live oak. The flora of Texas. It goes to extremes, just like Jordan, and though it is taken for granted that I will be impressed by extremes, I am not.

Country clubs are white wicker madhouses.

I have been scrutinized.

It is not perfectly clear that I have been brought down here at all for Jordan's possible physical delectation, but instead for close examination by his set, as they say. We've been members of the same set since—how long has it been? high school? grammar school? haven't we, Jordan? Jordan smiles and twirls his moustache.

Poor Jordan. Jordan's moustache is an affectation. Some men can get away with certain affectations, just as some women can get away with bleaching their hair. But Jordan doesn't really have the guts to go all the way with the suave man bit. So his anomalous moustache just grows and grows and he works on it day after day (the twirling part may be a genuine habit already) but his sideburns are cowardly and he is just miserable trying to carry it all off.

I had never thought much of people being part of a set before. Just dishes. But these people are really part of a set, dishes or people, it makes little difference. They're made of the same stuff, they wear the same emblems, cashmere and silk, vicuna and trips and toys and family concerns.

Today I was scrutinized by a woman named Madge. She is definitely one of Jordan's set and has been since high school. She invited us to have lunch with her at the golf club, and I didn't know what she wanted to have lunch at the golf club for, so I agreed to go with Jordan. She wanted to have lunch at the golf club so she could demonstrate how important she was at the golf club and how elegant her tastes were and how very much Jordan thought of her opinions. Her opinion of me is not very high, that much is certain.

I counted the knots between the pearls in her choker. That was the most pleasant available occupation. There was nothing in their conversation for me. Jordan has apparently told everyone that I am very brilliant and artistic and, therefore, likely to be a little on the eccentric side. Nothing is really further from the truth. Jordan is obtuse if he cannot understand that, but he may not. I take refuge in eccentricity when it is the only feasible course of action. Usually I do not find it necessary to appear eccentric or preoccupied. I would much rather soak in the immediacy of time and place and the people around, but when none of these are beautiful, I must retreat. It is easier doing this, I have found, than being nasty or curt and then explaining to myself and others later. And I always have to.

There were, by my estimate (since I could not see the back of Madge's neck) eighty-three knots in her choker.

She did not address herself to me, except to say hellohownicetomeetyou and goodbyehownicetomeetyou. Madge talked of the ballet and of old friends I did not know and what was new at Neiman's and divorces, hers and others.

Our table cloth at the golf club had a frayed southeastern corner.

On the way back from the golf club Jordan indulged me in a pure whim. I wanted to stop and ride a merry-go-round in a tiny amusement park. There seem to be a lot of them here. We stopped and I chose a grey horse. Jordan did not ride. Jordan plays polo, Madge said, but Jordan would not ride the horse next to me, which was vacant. He watched, looking very embarrassed.

Jordan does not know enough even to know what he should be

embarrassed about and what he should enjoy. Jordan would stand out in the rain.

For all the amusement parks they seem to have, it is odd that there is no brass ring. It must be a geographic matter. I was at the mercy of Jordan's embarrassment and we left the park after only one ride.

In the car he told me that whites do not go to that kind of park in Texas unless one is taking children. The parks are for and by the Mexicans. He says Messcans. He does not like the Messcans, but I have heard him say he admires the way the Messcan men treat their women.

It would be very difficult thinking my own thoughts if I belonged to him.

The cat is looking in at me again. He finds me more interesting than I find him, and the only reason I look at him at all is that he presents himself so obviously before my window. If I am to see anything at all, I must see him too—unless I press my nose up against the glass at the far edge of the window, the opposite edge from where he happens to be. The cat has apparently finally finished with the lizard. I cannot see it anywhere. No, wait, he has something curled up in his front claw. He drops it and I see it is the limp carcass of the lizard, its tail partway broken off.

He thinks that he is bringing the lizard back to life, tossing it around like that, playing with it.

He pretends he has something there.

Does he really think it is trying to elude him?

There are in the neighborhood of three thousand framed and glassed-in photographs of family, friends, pets, trips, graduations, weddings, babies, birthday parties, bon voyages, and more of the same. They are lining the walls of this den, as it is known in this house.

I am searching among the pictures. Mother and Dad at Amalfi. Sister on Graduation Day, white hat and robe. Mother and Dad in a Gondola. Brother Skiing in Gstaad. New Year's Eve at the Golf Club. Same decor, fifteen years ago. Brother Getting Ph.D. The Same Baby. 247 times. The Zeitgeist.

It has an alarming coherence, when displayed like this. The cycles of fashion are visible. The upward and onward. The growth of intellect, the accumulation of culture, the winning of honors, the consumption. The Commodore's Trophy. Mother Winning the Dominoes Tournament on the SS *Italia.* Dad Winning the Eleuthera Limbo Contest. Brother with his Swordfish. Babies. The Perpetuation of the Faith. First Communions. Knowing What It's All About.

I am looking among all the pictures for something special. Examining them. They are under my closest scrutiny. I have assumed the role of bitch at the golf club. These pictures are nobody. I am looking for Jordan's ex-wife. Someone always standing close to him, someone with long hair, someone dependent. I do not know for a fact that Jordan has ever been married. He has never told me that he was, but I cannot imagine someone as confident of himself as Jordan not being married and as self-centered not having been divorced.

Jordan asks me what I am doing looking at all the pictures so carefully. I tell him I am an amateur phrenologist.

I wish it were true. I wish this were not.

I know none of the rules of dominoes. Sorry.

I know none of the rules of polite conversation with this kind of person. I am not sure that there can be polite conversation with this kind of person, except on his own terms, or hers. I am sure that there can be calm and businesslike talk. I am sure that we can civilly discuss, admiringly, the quality of one's copper gutters on one's quality house. I know for a fact that the optimal graces of one's speaker system can be discussed, from several altogether practical standpoints, including the most practical of all, economical. I know that the land around us can be discussed, not for the beauty of its timber or its quietness, but in its economic and historic context: that it is the real legacy of the queen bee herself, and that over the years it has been a buffer in times of tribulation.

I have not yet met the commodore and his wife. I am tiring of the mental rehearsals.

Outside I walk among the liriope and know that things are essentially silken and wonderful. That streams are the truth and that fish and mayflies know it. That there is wisdom among the bamboo stalks everyone tries to kill. If I do not translate, it is my own shortcoming. I have been given the dictionary, a rare volume: Nature-Mind and Mind-Nature, complete with Irregular Verbs. If I can make no sense of it, it is my problem.

But it is not my problem. I have never had any trouble translating. For myself. I think I have understood the xylem and the phloem of the elms. I think with time I could understand the courting of the live oaks. What the meandering of a cat's eyes while he sleeps means. The shapes of clouds keep the narrative viable.

The liriope is about to come into flower. Spikes are shooting up the center of each planting; then there will be the little blue flowers I have never seen but have seen pictures of and have read about. There will at least be some kind of flower. These certainties are comforting. But the liriope is a very special kind of grass, and I think Jordan or his mother or whoever it is here who would get flustered about these things would get flustered if they saw me walking in the liriope. I saw the cat jumping from liriope clump to liriope clump, and he seemed to enjoy it. I think Jordan would be very stingy to disallow me this small enjoyment. I do not think Jordan himself could do any better than to walk among the liriope with me, but I do not think Jordan will ever know it. If only he could consult the flowers and the muds in the bayous and the cypress trunks.

Think about it, Jordan.

It's not all that obscure.

Just think in terms of you and me. That shouldn't overtax your mind.

What we have is what some people call a relationship.

That's what some people call it.

I call it foolishness, a waste of time for both of us.

And you, here among the Spanish moss, pretending to be courting me. If I were given to hysterics, I would laugh.

I have noticed that there are two distinct kinds of Spanish moss.

You, among your golf club set, pretending to show me off. But wondering.

You, puttering around your mother's kitchen, impressing me with your bachelor cooking. Jordan, it's supposed to be the other way around.

If you could think about the message of the liriope and Spanish oaks and cypress through all the nights they have practiced being. And then tell me what you think.

I am no better.

I should have better sense.

It should not have gotten to this point. I should have said no the first time. I should have, but I was lonely. Loneliness can be lovely, but only for a time. That should have been it. It wasn't. You had flair, I told myself. You thought you had flair, I thought to myself.

It hasn't been worth the effort, Jordan. Better now than ten years from now.

I found out today in the tone of your mother's voice. Nothing she said. She knows better. The tone. I won't sound like that.

I would rather watch the cat weave through the doorway and mark it with his muzzle. First one side, then the other.

The cat, whom I find odious and beastly, is at least true to what's inside him. He is his only commitment.

Do dominoes players have commitments?

Jordan tells me he believes I am placing entirely too much emphasis on the cat incident. The one where the cat killed the lizard. For nothing.

Jordan believes, he told me today, that I am a pantheist. Or perhaps just a deist. He would not explain the difference. I am not sure he could.

Jordan tells me cats often kill for sport. It is their way of enjoying themselves, he says.

I don't think anybody should enjoy killing. I don't think anybody should kill, under any circumstances. When I was small I used to have nightmares about having unintentionally killed someone, and then I was shut away in prison for the rest of my life. There was no explaining.

There was no liriope, no Texas morning like a bathroom full of steam.

So I have met Jordan's parents, and they have met me. They are not mine.

I have met Jordan's mother and analyzed the timbre and resonance of her voice. I shall not forget it.

I have met Jordan's father, the commodore, and he is a photograph.

Jordan has taken the cat to the bayou, tied a rope and a brick around its neck, and drowned it.

He told me he thought the cat upset me too much, it was better this way, and it was after all just a cat.

Today I am leaving and should have left long ago, should never have come except without coming I would not have seen the lizard die a mysterious death on the claws of the cat, would not have seen liriope spikes and two kinds of Spanish moss, hanging and ball, would not have known what strong presences those broad cypress are; would not have felt dead heat stop me or shivered at the ripples mayflies cause on the bayou; questioned the souls of all the departed oysters whose shells make roads and roadbeds, why? These roads are the whitest anywhere. And there is no more silent sand anywhere than on Padre, where hawks and rattlers and mice and all are ghostly figments, as this is a ghostly figment, until, like all hawks and snakes, cats and oysters and lizards, it can be seen and recognized.

Jordan I see you.

The Pump

His quid sinks into the middle of the gooseberry bush. Granpa never misses.

He hands me a warm quarter and smiles from inside his old blue eyes. "A pack of Mail Pouch and a plug of Horseshoe," he says and starts circling his pocketknife on the dished-out stone in his left hand. Then he looks up and sees me still here. "Oh-oh. Almost forgot," he says, trying to fool me. "Bet you'd like some of that paper ribbon candy." He reaches into the big soft pocket in his pinchecks and pulls out a penny. "For your errand," he explains. He goes back to sharpening his knife and calls out after me, "Not so fast, sweetheart, or you'll skin that knee again." Granpa always calls me sweetheart. My name's the same as Granma's was, but just before I was born she died.

Granpa knows how big I feel running up to the corner for him to Paul's Variety Store. They have all kinds of candy there and only two kinds of chewing tobacco, though they used to have Yankee Girl too. The candy is just inside the door, and Paul's Store is right on the way home for kids from Union School, which is one way from our house, and St. Mary's, which is the other. Sometimes the school kids stop and eat candy on our front retaining wall under the trees, but Daddy says they leave paper all over the yard and if he sees them he will chase them. Paul's has a few other things, like ice cream that Ike Paul packs by hand into little goldfish cartons and popsicles and fudgesicles and dixiecups that you eat with a wooden stick, but they're always vanilla. Mama sometimes sends me to get canned goods, like green beans, or bread, but mostly I get chewing tobacco for Granpa.

Once upon a time Granpa was a big-league baseball player. Everybody in town knows that, everybody knows who he is; everybody when I tell them my name asks if I am related to Granpa. Then I tell them yes I am, and we have a trunk full of baseballs and mothballs and Granpa's old wool uniforms up in our attic. When I go help Phillips get something down out of the attic—like the black summer fans that turn slowly and hum in the night, something like that—then I sometimes go look at the big nest of baseballs in the trunk. They are all written on, and there are scrap books in there too with newspaper clippings and old telegrams, like the ones about Granpa pitching the day Daddy was born. Daddy says the written-on baseballs are really special, that one was the last ball for Granpa's no-hitter and the men who signed were on his teams, the Indians and the Browns and the Senators. There are some plain hardballs someplace else, but girls don't play. Daddy gave some of the hardballs to my best cousin Luke. And that's why I have to go get the tobacco, because Granpa was a pitcher.

When I get back Granpa will be right there where he was. He always is. He keeps a campstool, the little wooden kind with a canvas seat, right outside the door on the back porch. "Let's go find us a spot," he'll say every nice morning, and most are nice now that summer's coming. And then we'll go find us a spot out under the elms and maybe I'll swing on the bright green swing he and Daddy put up for me and that Granpa paints the same bright green when spring comes every year. One very tall elm grows close to the house, one with branches starting way way up, and that is the one the swing is on. I can't see how they ever got the chains on and I don't remember if I did see. Maybe Daddy had to climb up with a long ladder or maybe he threw the chains across from the porch roof. The chains have gotten rusty though and sometimes if I haven't swung for a while, my hands get orange. Some days I will draw with a stick in the dust under the swing or maybe gather sticks for Granpa to whittle. But whatever I do, Granpa does the same thing, chew and whittle and chew and spit and sing me old songs.

When I go to Paul's these days I don't go the easy way, not right around the front of the house to the front walk and down the long steps there to the sidewalk and then left, straight up the street to Paul's on the other corner of our block. That's the way I used to go when I was younger, when I just learned how to go to Paul's by myself. Sometimes Mama would send me right out the front door so it would be even easier. There are better ways to get to Paul's, and I am always finding more of them. When I get better on my bike, I have another way figured out on the back alley along the railroad tracks. Mama says she doesn't want me walking back there. There might be bums there, she says. Once a bum came to our house from the tracks and asked for food and Mama gave it to him, but he had to eat on the lawntable. Daddy found out and got mad. They'll mark our house, he yelled, and threw the evening *Advocate* up on the cupboard in a tent. I looked but never saw any marks. But Mama says not to borrow trouble so I go on the other alley, the one that cuts our block in two. I get there by going through the nextdoor back yard, where my great-grandmother and Aunt Beck and Miss Graham, their boarder, live, and then turn down the alley straight out to Main Street and then left and two more houses then Paul's. The alley is paved with rounded old bricks, and on the other side of it lives the Italian shoemaker with the beautiful flowers, then the Lehrers who have twins you can't tell apart, and then Paul's. Once I went through the Italian's fence and the Lehrers' back yard, but I didn't come out right.

"What for you, missy?" fat old Ike Paul asks me.

"Tobacco for Granpa, Mail Pouch and Horseshoe plug, please." I get out the quarter. Ike goes to the other front corner of the store, away from the door and the candy, and opens a special breadbox that says "Beech Nut" on it and gets out a paper pouch of cut tobacco and the hard little brown plug all wrapped in its cellophane. "Getting low," Ike Paul says. "Better put in an order." We trade. "Anything else?" he wants to know.

"You got any ribbon candy?" I ask, knowing that he does. I saw when I came in. He goes over to the candy case, huffing and puffing, and draws out a box with the coil of paper with its bright colored dots.

"Right here you are," he says. "How much?"

It is a game we play, Ike and me. "Penny's worth," I tell him, though he already knows Granpa gave me a penny for the errand. I watch Ike carefully as he unrolls the coil, counting the changes of color with his fat fingers. He reaches back into the candy case for his scissors and snips off my purchase.

"Need a bag?" says Ike.

I say no and we trade again, and I run home up the alley streaming colored dots of sugar in the wind.

"Well looky here," Granpa says. "What you got now?"

I give him his two kinds of tobacco and he spits out some juice toward the gooseberry bush because he doesn't like gooseberries or gooseberry bushes either one. "That's a good girl." Granpa undoes the top of the Mail Pouch, pulls out a pinch, and sticks it in the side of his mouth. "Nice and fresh," he says. "How's old Ike doing?"

"He's ok. But he's almost out of your tobacco. Says he's going to put in another order for you."

"Good old Ike," says Granpa. "I remember Ike when he was your age." I try to imagine Ike my age, but he is so big and fat I can't. Granpa goes on with his whittling and chewing.

I have Suzy outside, since Rove had to be put to sleep, and in fact I left her on the swing when I went to get Granpa his tobacco. I think about going to get her some clothes and playing dolls this morning when Granpa surprises me.

"Luke is coming over," he says. "Mama and Zet are going to St. Louis shopping and we're going to have a high old time for ourselves." Luke is a year younger than me, but he's ok. He doesn't act like a baby, like some kids who are five. So I say, "Good."

But Granpa is full of surprises today.

"I thought we would pump the well out. It's time, and I just haven't gotten around to it. I need some help." Granpa has trouble breathing and has two raw eggs in a milkshake every day. Pumping out the well is a big job. Last year it took all day, but the water is worth it.

So until Luke gets here I need to do something, I'm so excited. Granpa maybe needs some sticks to whittle. Granpa doesn't whittle anything, I mean he doesn't carve a statue or anything out of the wood. All we have here is tiny twigs from the elms mostly, and they break at the joints. Granpa showed me one day how to break elm twigs at the joints and I spent the whole morning breaking them at those little knuckles. I never saw the knuckles before that, and now that's the first thing I see. Granpa keeps his pocket knife sharp, for whittling and for cutting his plug. After he whittles a while, he'll pull up the loose pincheck blue trousers into a kind of fold and then wipe his knife clean and get his plug out of his shirt pocket and cut off a little piece and pop it in his mouth like a piece of candy. It doesn't taste like candy though. I tried it once. Not even the plug, the shredded. I spit it out fast, and the plug is supposed to be worse. That's what Granpa says. So I am busy gathering Granpa some twigs and sticks, trying to find some bigger ones because those are the ones he likes best. Granpa does what he calls just plain whittling and what he does is make a point on the stick and then sharpen it some more and some more and some more until the stick is just about all gone. Between Granpa's feet the pile of little white chips grows and grows, and finally when the whittling stick is too little to hold and whittle any more, Granpa breaks it, so little girls don't get hurt, he says.

"Granpa, were you really a doctor?" I ask. Like with Ike, this is a game. It is an old question.

"I went through medical school, if that's what you mean," Granpa says, just like always.

"But I mean did you have an office and give people shots and make them well?" I hate Dr. Strange, my pediatrician. He gave me a cold shot and I got pneumonia and he makes everybody get undressed, even Luke, cause Luke told me. I like the nurse better because she keeps the candy.

"No, sweetheart. I never was that kind of doctor."

"Because you played baseball."

"That's right. Either had to go play ball or be a decent doctor. Couldn't be both." Granpa chews a couple more times. "I was young," he says.

"You had to go to spring training, isn't that right?"

"Every spring there was trouble. 'Look here,' they'd say to me, 'either you want to be a doctor or you want to play ball.' But I'd get caught up somehow and then your grandmother and I got married and I loved to pitch."

"Daddy says nobody could catch you."

"Your daddy exaggerates. He had just as good an arm himself. But I learned a lesson."

Somehow the story has gotten off the track because Granpa seems sad. Something went wrong with the story. "But Gabby Street on the radio says nobody had a fastball like you."

Granpa whittles a couple more licks and chews and thinks and finally says, "'Cause I was so tall." Granpa is still whittling and thinking and I am still wishing I could say something to make him stop when Zetta and Luke pull up the drive in her new turquoise blue

Studebaker Land Cruiser.

"Some buggy you got there, Zet," Granpa calls out, sounding happy again.

"Thanks, Pa," Zetta says. Everybody calls Granpa "Pa"—except me and Luke—even if he isn't theirs.

Out jumps Luke with a new puzzle and a hardball bulging in his jacket pocket. Luke is always getting puzzles, it seems to me, and learns fast how to work them and then comes over and says to me, "Betcha can't get this one." He hands me a small coiled spring with a little circle of metal caught in one of the loops of the spring. "You gotta get the ring off without going to the end. Can you?" he wants to know.

"Now where'd you come up with that, Lukey-boy," Granpa says. "I haven't seen one of those for years."

"Dad says now the war's over they can start making things like this. I'm going to get an American Flyer for Christmas."

"That's a long way off, Luke," I say. "Maybe you'll be bad."

Luke turns his head so Granpa can't see and sticks his fat old tongue right out at me.

"Catch me a few, Granpa?" Luke draws one of the plain balls from the attic out of the bulging pocket. He runs backward on the lawn until he reaches the middle of the back yard.

"Ok," Granpa says, "but easy now. Don't want you fireballing 'em at me and me with no glove." I don't think Luke can really fireball, but he is making a real study of baseball cards. Pitchers in particular.

Luke's all right, for a boy. Of all my cousins, I see him the most, almost every day. He and Zetta and Ted only live about four blocks away. "Hardly worth getting the car out of the garage," Zetta will say if she drives over to our house. Or Mama will say the same thing if she is the one to drive over to Zetta's. Zetta's used to be Mama's house, before I was born, before Granma died and left Granpa all alone in the big house and he made Daddy bring Mama and come live with him. It just so happened that Zetta and Ted needed a house then so they got Mama's old one. But before all that, even Granpa and Granma lived there. When Daddy was just a little boy. I've seen pictures of him on the cellar door over there and hanging around the corner downspout.

You ask Luke what he wants to be and he has two answers. A doctor and a baseball player. Or a baseball player and a doctor. *And*, not *or*. Granpa keeps telling Luke you can't really be both, but Luke thinks maybe he can.

"Let's see what you got for a change-up, Lukey," Granpa calls out to the middle of the grass.

Luke plants his feet, peers toward Granpa, goes into a windup, and throws. I can't see any difference, and I wonder if Granpa can. "Fine, Luke; fine, boy." Granpa spits at the gooseberry bush and flips the ball back to Luke. "Watch for the signal and you tell me what you see."

"Two?" says Luke like he can't believe it. "I don't know how."

"'Member how I showed you to hold the ball?"

Luke nods.

"Now just ease up a bit on your fastball and try spinning it. We'll just see what happens," Granpa says. "You got a natural break, boy."

Luke beams and goes into the windup. The ball goes into the chips at Granpa's feet. "Well, hot-damn," says Granpa, who never talks like that. "A sinker! You may not have a curve, but you've got a sinker. I'll be."

"It did; it did," is all Luke can say. He can hardly stand still.

"You just remember how you did that one and you'll be in good shape. Now let's do it again, 'fore you forget."

"We won't be gone long, Pa," Mama says as she and Zetta come out the back porch screen door. "Just going to pick up a few things at Stix and maybe run over to Famous if there's time. We'll park at the Market—anything you want special from there?" I am glad Luke and I are not going. I hate the Union Market Garage with its long scary ramps, all dark, and its old rattly elevator that takes you down to the first floor. And when you get there, to the market itself, all the butchers' stalls and headcheese and blutwurst and cow heads in the case and on the wall with fur and horns still and the insides and all and the salty smell of the place. It is terrible. I don't even like to go to St. Louis at all. The car makes me sick because Luke and I are always trying to read in the back seat. Comics. "Just look at the scenery," Mama will say, but I never can for very long. The only part of the scenery I like is the top of the bluffs. The rest isn't nice.

"Not that I can think of," Granpa says, "unless you see a nice piece of Hunter's braunschweiger. We're going to have our own fresh vegetables before long." Granpa knows Mama will bring home bags of fresh oranges anyway. He looks down to the field of three lots behind our house and yard. He and Daddy have planted all kinds of vegetables there, kinds I didn't even know about, like swiss chard.

And the rhubarb that comes back wider and wider, Granpa says, every year, and the strawberries and melons and I don't know what all. "You girls just run along and have a good time. Don't rush getting back. We've got our day cut out for us—we got a well to pump out."

"Well, I think we'll have lunch in the Tea Room and be back about two or two-thirty, and Phillips will make sandwiches for you." Zetta is already in the car and she starts it as Mama gets in. "Be good children for Pa," Mama says, and the Land Cruiser coasts quietly down the drive. Zetta beeps goodbye as they turn right and start down the side street for the highway.

Luke runs to the end of the yard where there is a clump of iris just before the embankment. He stands leaning out, waving at the car as it disappears over the railroad tracks and around a bend in the street.

When he comes back, Luke throws Granpa about three million sinkers, but finally Granpa remembers the well. Suzy, my friend, falls off the swing when I try to swing her, and the two of us won't fit. I am thinking and scuffing my toes in the dust under the swing. "Hew-ee, Luke," Granpa says. "I'm done. You're going to throw that arm away, young fellow like you."

Luke looks as though he is glad to have a reason to stop. "Thanks, Granpa," Luke says.

I start picking my way across the chat drive to the pump. Daddy just put down fresh white chat this spring, and it hasn't worked down flat into the dirt yet. I don't like the white chat because it's so pointy. The brown is rounder. You can even ride a bike on the brown, but Daddy likes the white. Granpa goes and gets a little rag from somewhere in the outside basement steps and goes over the pump with it, getting all the dust and specks of rust off.

"We're going to take turns," Granpa says. "Who goes first?"

Luke jumps up and down and says, "Oh, me! Me!" and since he's younger and company it's ok.

Granpa gets his little oil can out of his pocket, although I didn't know he had it hidden in there, and gives the joints a couple of squirts. Then Granpa goes over to the hose and gets a pan of water and is ready to prime.

"Holy Cow," says Luke, straining at the pump handle.

"Wait a minute, wait a minute," Granpa says. "I better start it." Granpa has had his two-egg milkshake, so it's probably all right. He has such skinny long hands and he breathes hard most of the time.

But pretty soon the pump is loosened up and primed and going like sixty, and Granpa lets Luke take over. "She's all yours," he says, and he gets his campstool under him just in time.

Luke and I are pumping as hard as we can and taking turns and every once in a while Granpa will come and pump real fast and see how much water comes out. The water is still coming out in a fat stream, and I think Luke might be getting tired of this, but I tell him it was just like this last year and we're glad he's here to help us because Granpa and I could never get it done by ourselves. That makes Luke pump harder and harder and when Phillips comes out on the back porch to call us for lunch, we're all glad. Granpa has been mopping his forehead all morning with the handkerchief and breathing hard and chewing tobacco and singing. Luke and I have been talking about how good the well water will taste when it gets pumped out all nice and clean, and Phillips says, "That's right. There's nothing like sweetwater from a well." It is a rule that nobody takes a drink of well water before the well gets pumped out, because Granpa says it's dirty water. It doesn't look dirty. I tried it. It doesn't taste dirty either, just sweet like Phillips says, and I didn't get sick.

So at the kitchen table we eat toasted cheese and toasted hamsalad and sweet baby pickles, and Luke and I get milk to drink and Granpa and Phillips drink iced tea and soon we are back outside pumping. "Won't be long the sun will be around over here," Granpa says squinting through the cover of elm leaves. It is Luke's turn and he is pumping steadily and the stream of water is getting thinner. I am back on the swing, not really swinging. Just sitting and thinking and dangling my feet in the dust, drawing little things with my toes, patting out footprints, the swing moving just a little. A breeze has started up. Granpa looks over to the west to see what kinds of clouds we are getting. The clouds look friendly. I wish it were really summer and Luke and I could collect locust shells and line them up like little soldiers.

"Sweetheart, look at that poor Luke," Granpa says and startles me a little when he says it. "Luke, your tongue's hanging out, boy. Don't you know enough to ask for your relief pumper?" Across the pointy white chat I come, and Luke sits down on the vent pipe from the well. It is in the concrete platform too, with the pump in the middle, and the vent, with its little cap with holes in it, is just the other side of the pump from the handle. Sometimes, when Luke and I were little, we put twigs down the holes and little rocks, but now we know better. "How's the arm, Luke?" Granpa asks.

"I wasn't really tired, Granpa," Luke says, breathing hard.

The stream is really getting littler and littler and soon the well will be pumped dry. Granpa is whittling and singing us his funny old songs with lots of verses and chewing his tobacco. I used to wonder how he could sing with his mouth full of tobacco and spit, but he told me how he just tucks the tobacco up alongside his gum like a chipmunk. It makes his face look lopsided a little, but he can sing without taking the tobacco out. I tried it with gum and it works.

Granpa gets up from his campstool and goes to the garage. It is a big garage, with room for four cars because it is the garage for two houses, ours and Grandmama and Beck's. Aunt Beck has a Chrysler that she never drives and Granpa gave Mama a Packard for Christmas and Daddy has the blue pickup he uses to go to the mines and hunting and then there's a funny old black car that belonged to Uncle Will who died and the doors open backwards. And that fills up the garage except that there is really a lot of room left over for shelves with paint and garden tools and lots of old things, a horse collar even, so many things I haven't seen them all. Granpa is going after the paint. Pretty soon here he comes with a half-gallon of Sherwin-Williams Aluminum swinging by its wire handle. I can hardly keep up the pumping while he pries the lid up and starts to work on the skin. "I think this is through, Granpa," I tell him, though there is still a trickle of water coming. "Can I quit now?"

"Just a bit more," Granpa says. "I'll let you paint the vent if you get it really dry." That is all I need. Luke is over on the lawn catching pop-ups from a make-believe batter. The sun is getting close to the well. I think I can see it moving up the driveway. I pump and pump and finally when I can get no more water, I turn to Granpa who has the paint all stirred and ready and the narrow paintbrush in his hand. "Let's see," he says and gives the handle a few smart pumps and nothing comes out, I am glad to see. "Dry as bone," he says. "Let's get her painted up."

Granpa is a quick painter and neat, too. Luke's pop flies are tearing down elm leaves and coming back to earth in surprising places. When Granpa paints he doesn't drip. He does the top of the pump and then the long curved handle and then the main part of the pump and then takes out his rag and dries carefully around the spout and paints that part too. When he is finished, the sun isn't yet all the way to the well top. "Here you go," Granpa says, and he hands me the brush with the silver paint. Only the tips of the bristles are wet with silver and I know that pretty soon there will be silver paint running down the handle and everything. I paint round and round and round the pipe with the silver paint and soon it is all done except for the cap, and I see Luke watching.

"Here, Luke, you want to do the top?"

Luke's big brown eyes grow as round as saucers and he takes the sticky paint brush. He paints the top very carefully and doesn't even get any down the holes. Then after Granpa gets the turpentine and gets us all cleaned up, he fishes in the soft pocket of his trousers again and says, "We need something from the store." He hands us each a warm nickel and says, "Something cold," and we hug him tight almost off his campstool and start a running race for Paul's ice cream freezer. Just before we turn onto the brick alley on the other side of Grandmama's, I turn and look back at Granpa. He sits under the elm tree there on his campstool, and he gives the gooseberry bush a spit and whittles some more. The sun is starting on one corner of the well top when the trees blow just right.

Gravity

On one of his quadrille pads she has scribbled her kind of scientific note: Of the differences in the paths of falling leaves. Of primitives.

Here is recorded how the elm leaf turns over and over, yellow in the sham summer day of autumn. Of the oaks it is said that their leaves are like clean, timeless sheets of paper. Of the catalpa, how its leaves meander side to side, the broadest face of all to the air below, resistance creating resistance. It is the oldest story on earth and always ends the same: Irresistible force (earth, leaf), please meet immovable object (leaf, earth). But, she remembers, no reflections. Just raw data. Science.

Well then, details of the dainty maple, spiralling on the axis of its stem, drilling the air, a visual echo of the maple seed's twin green wings in spring. On the quadrille grid she reconstructs the equation of elms cut in mid-summer. No one has told the seeds in their paper cases that they are the seeds of doom. They will volunteer next year, and in the autumn's garden beds they sleep the sleep of hope. Final note: the great slow oak, the acorn, which drops directly.

Across the street, a white-haired man in tweeds sweeps the first of fall from his entry. Puffing on his prize meerschaum, he is autumn at ease. In this village an ordinance forbids the burning of leaves.

In the den her husband reads. A spiral of wire leads from his headphones to the blue glow of the tuner. He has become a puzzle to her, as perhaps she has to him. She knows neither what goes on in his head nor to what he is listening. Vivaldi. Willie Nelson. Anything, but nothing by halves. The attraction is still there, still mutual.

All inhabitants are fed, all dishes are done. She does her best to have them live in a clock of a house. All floors are waxed, surfaces free of dust, offspring sleeping or feigning sleep, beds otherwise made to be unmade to be made. The clothing is clean, insofar as that is possible. Each day the dirty laundry descends to the basement via the chute. The next day these soiled items rise from the earth as if lighter than air, seeking their rightful places, defying gravity, blasted off by chlorines and phosphates.

She notes that man measures his advancement by his ability to defy the laws of nature.

She pushes one switch, ON. She pushes another, RUN PROGRAM.

It is evening and she is alone. She holds a small hand calculator and inserts a narrow strip of magnetically encoded plastic. The machine hums it through its card reader. The program emerges from the other side of the calculator. The display lights up, CRD. She turns the card over and feeds its second side to the machine.

Feeding the machine reminds her of the two supposedly sleeping children. The younger, a boy, does not like school, or so he claims. He worries too much about his image, and she worries that he is too young to let images get in the way of the truth. And how can someone five years old hate half the human race, as he claims to. Daily it grows more difficult telling what is real with him. With the girl, it's easy. To her, her daughter's deceptions are transparent, though that may be because their deceptions are the same. Her husband finds his daughter otherwise. Her school cannot measure her, since she falls in the 99th percentile in everything and whenever possible soars off the top end of the scale into space. She probably finds her mother obtuse. Daughters always do. They aren't able to measure the boy either, how much he's playing for laughs. Before bed, he told of flying in the night, of just taking off from his windowsill. Of course, she told him. When you're older and can borrow grandpa's plane.

You're older, she tells herself. It's all right for you to do what you want. No one can ask any questions. Enjoy yourself. Take it easy. Relax. Play a game.

"The Lunar Landing Game," announces the calculator's manual. She never can remember the instructions.

"You are 350 feet off the surface of the moon, descending at a rate of 50 feet per second. The display will count down from 3, and when it reaches 0, you have 1 second in which to enter an even number of pounds of fuel to burn."

She knows if she manages to land safely, it will be only a matter of sheer luck and blind instinct. But if she does, does it matter how?

The fall wind is negligible, just as on the moon's surface there are no winds. The autumn has already done its due on the maples and box elders. The oaks' top branches cling tightly to their leaves, and she suddenly recalls seeing crowns of leaves on the oaks in the snow. In the night a siren wails, but this is not the season for tornados. In the street in front of their house a loud car rushes past, and it turns at the corner, screeching. Behind it comes the village police, siren, red light.

STOP, the calculator says. GO. It counts the seconds her space capsule falls, down, down, the surface of the moon coming up, up. 3-blink-blink, 2-blink-*think*, 1-think-think. Oh, what the hell, she says out loud, and punches 7.

What elms remain and the maples went first. As long as she can remember she has been a watcher of elms, starting with the twenty-some that shrouded her grandpa's house, deep green all summer and diamond ice all winter. Now afternoons across the street the white-haired man rakes what oak leaves his trees have given him, leading his harvest toward a meager windrow. For all she knows the old man knows everything there is to know. At the moment she cannot even think of his name, or if she ever knew it. Her son yells at him: Hey, Poopoo! and she hopes he has not heard. It appears he has not, and she wonders: Is yelling *hey poopoo* in the nature of boys as not appearing to have heard is in the nature of white-haired old men as falling is in the nature of leaves?

For the moment that question seems remote. She has just crashed on the lunar surface. The owner's manual continues: "To restart the game, enter A′. To stop the game, enter B′. The game may only be stopped for 5 seconds, but if the player wishes to resume more quickly, again enter A′."

The man in the next room listening to secret music, her husband, wrestles with a problem so complex only a handful of scientists realize it exists. In fact, it is one of his professional duties to create problems so that others may solve them. No wonder they have their days, she thinks. He brings home with him a portable computer terminal ("Sensitive Item: Property of U.S. Government" says its sticker) so he can use it at night. Night is the time when the big computer at the lab is not overwhelmed with jobs that have to be done last month. What does a person who makes notes on the falling paths of leaves do with one who orders the unorderable, thinks the unthinkable, solves the unknown with a sensitive item? Other than make love.

ERROR, accuses her lunar landing display. Oh please, she thinks, tell me something I don't know. She switches the damned machine off, erases the program. The machine knows nothing now. It will not know anything until she tells it.

The white-haired man across the street knows something. He rakes now that he will not be forced to rake so much later. He knows it is silly to calculate for a wind, which might as easily sweep the leaves away from him as sweep all his neighbors' leaves onto his yard. He accepts as a primitive the concept of gravity, he assumes its continuity. Mobility is not in the vocabulary of his life, does not even occur to him, was unheard of, in his generation. Oak man. Man long standing. By comparison we are the green ash, the silver maples flitting about. Fast growing. Shallow rooted.

Can anyone here calculate the value of *G*?

Her husband has removed the headphones and quieted the mind of the FM receiver. Now he brings the terminal, the size of an attache case and of an inconsequential grey color, to her desk. Where the quadrille paper is. Only it is about to be displaced. His portable terminal hooks into the main computer through the telephone. On the back of the terminal are two grey rubber cups called acoustical couplers, where the phone receiver fits. Otherwise the sensitive item looks like any electric typewriter.

He speaks: "May I use your phone. The kids are on mine." He already has the cover off the terminal and is plugging the three-prong adapter into the outlet.

"I thought the kids were in bed."

"No, Kitsy is talking to Lisa. Look, I can't sit around all day waiting in a queue for a job to be processed. I've got other things to do. Would you go grocery shopping at five o'clock?"

He has such a way with analogies, she thinks. "You know, your questions somehow aren't."

"Aren't what?"

"Aren't questions."

"Will you quit it? This is important. I don't ask often."

"True." He never asks. He tells, he states.

"My terminal has to talk to John's or they won't know what they're supposed to be doing tomorrow."

"Just what the kids say."

"I knew you'd say that. That's why I said it. Now would you just move some of this junk."

"Those are papers, my notes on the leaves. This is my desk."

"Won't take long. Just a couple of flags and a few minor adjustments to our new subroutine."

Just what the kids say, she thinks again. He dials the number of the laboratory computer access station and snuggles the receiver into the couplers. READY, the terminal types, after he logs on with his code number and password. The machine tells him how much time he has used and how much time he has left. Together they go through the formalities of getting into the proper mode. He and the machine type at each other their coded dialogue of offs and ons, gates opening and shutting, counterfeiting thought. Yes-no, flip-flop. She wonders if there's really anything happening there, anything real.

When the fall rains came this afternoon, she inventoried on the quadrille pad the flora and fauna of the backyard. Someone before them here was crazy for maples, damn it. The maples are just about all they've got, and plenty of them. So many in fact she has named them. Today the crotch of the Bad Maple is stained black with fall's damp. The sides of its upstretched legs are dry, one of them green with a primitive growth of moss on its north side. The Spindly Maple is all wet, except for a small section near the base that is dry. A smear of unnatural green, a more mature moss, drips down its simple pillar. High in the Complicated Maple the ragged fat rope of a years-ago swing diminishes each winter. The tree is open to the rawest of weather, far from the house. Next year, she thinks, we must get them all, the named and the unnamed, trimmed properly. Pausing on one of the branches, a squirrel clutches at the air before it, as if to keep from falling. Dead ferns collapse into themselves and feed their rhizomes with last summer's fodder. The fir seedling they planted by the barbeque pit has grown to an even shade of green, braced for the snow. And on and on. Fall in the suburbs. Tonight the leaves are soggy on the ground, the air is full of mist, and the wet streets hiss all day, all night.

But one more data point for the quadrille pad. This afternoon while she was taking inventory, just outside her window a bird flew down. At the same time, from nowhere another bird flew up. She expected at any moment to see the birds collide in midair and somehow atomize, disintegrate in a cloud of feathers. She would see the face of energy itself. And just then the phone rang. "Tom Lawless," said the dynamo they used for a broker. "It's your lucky day," he said. "Consolidated Light came down. I got your 300 at 13."

Now the night wind picks up, moaning a low sound in the gutter at the ell where the kitchen and breakfast room come together. Though her husband's specialty of specialties is neither acoustics nor wind tunnels, he always says the moan has to do with the big overhang. From there he always swings into his standard twenty-minute declamation on how much better-built older houses are, from the scientific point of view.

Science be hanged, she thinks. Enough of reasons. When people are happy, reasons don't matter. People wear themselves out, make themselves miserable, just to be logical and exquisitely defensible. Anything that matters just finally is, like the old man, like the seasons circling and spiralling down time. Our defenses and our attacks will change those things not one bit.

The moan in the kitchen corner is joined by another. It is a siren, and it is coming closer. The siren is joined by still another. A red light flashes up their driveway, hitting the garage door. Again and again it paints the same swath across the door. Another wreck. She wonders: Why do people give cars to absolute children? Why do people hurry so? Why do people get tight and try to drive? She remembers: There had been no thud, no screech of brakes, no crash of metal against metal or headlight against tree.

She hurries to the front of the house. Stopped across the street is a red emergency vehicle from the village fire department and a white Arrow ambulance with a gold band around it. The beacons turn mutely, striping the neighborhood again and again. The ambulance doors are open. The firemen and paramedics have gone into the house across the street. She knows what has happened, that she should not watch, that she does not want to watch, yet she watches. On a stretcher the men bring the white-haired man wrapped fat in blankets, no face showing, out the front door, down the front stairs, out the walk through the oaks' newly fallen leaves.

By nothing more than a stir of air she knows her husband stands behind her now. When she reaches for his hand, she finds that he is reaching for hers. And though neither of them speaks, neither of them needs to as they both try to assemble the language of the leaves and of fall.

Born in St. Louis and educated at MacMurray College and the University of Illinois, Catherine Petroski now lives with her husband and two children in Durham, N.C., after stays in Austin, Texas, and Chicago. She has published in such magazines as *Ms., Prairie Schooner, Virginia Quarterly Review,* and most frequently, *North American Review.* Her stories have been recognized several times by the *Best American Short Stories* series and won the Texas Institute of Letters Short Fiction Prize. She has held the Bridgman Fiction Scholarship at Bread Loaf, a Yaddo fellowship, an Illinois Arts Council appointment as Writer-in-Residence, and in 1979 traveled in Britain, Germany, and Austria as an NEA Fellow.